# Hired by the Single Dad

## The Single Dads of Seattle

# Book 1

Whitley Cox

For Cora Seton.

A friend, a mentor, an inspiration.

# Contents

# Chapter 1

♥

"To divorce!"

"Hear, hear!"

"Good riddance!"                                                    '

Did somebody groan?

Mark Herron's interest piqued at the numerous cheers of the women behind him. Glasses clinked and giggles echoed around the big booth table at the posh bar, The Ludo Lounge, in downtown Seattle. He didn't dare turn around, at least not yet, but he tuned out the rest of the bar and zeroed in on the intriguing conversation going on just one table over.

Who celebrated divorce?

Certainly not him.

It had been one of the most horrible, gut-wrenching things he'd ever gone through. Not to mention the toll it had taken on Gabe. No, Mark's divorce from Cheyenne had been brutal.

But yet, these women appeared to be in celebration. At least some of them did.

It was certainly the place for it. Dark, big, deep booths, rocking music, a small dance floor and a price tag on even a glass of house wine high enough to keep out the hooligans who came just to get shit-faced and laid. It was a classy bar.

But that didn't mean you couldn't have a good time at a classy place, and that's exactly what these women sounded like they were after.

"Come on, Tori, celebrate," one woman encouraged. "He's gone for good."

"Yeah …" came a breathy, almost hesitant voice. "Gone for good." She didn't sound nearly as enthusiastic as the rest. "We're not *technically* divorced yet. I just filed for separation."

"Well, it's a start!" a third woman cheered.

"After he kicked me out," she murmured.

"Come on, you've got your whole life ahead of you now," came another friend. "Plenty of hot, single men in Seattle."

"That's right. Take life by the balls, chica." This woman sounded incredibly drunk. Mark could just picture her pantomiming grabbing a scrotum that hung precariously over their table. "The world is your oyster … speaking of, we should get some raw ones brought over to the table. They're an aphrodisiac, and we need to get Tori here *laid!*"

Mark cringed. Whoever this Tori was, his heart went out to her.

"I'm okay, guys, really," the same hesitant voice from earlier affirmed. "No aphrodisiacs needed. Nobody … at least not me … is going to be getting laid tonight. I'm taking a break."

"I don't think Ken is taking a break," the obnoxious oyster-loving friend said. "He couldn't even be faithful *during* your marriage. What makes you think he's taking a break now?"

"He's not. I know that he's with Nicole, the dental hygienist he was cheating on me with. His sister confirmed that Ken moved her in a few months ago."

"See! See! All the more reason for you to jump back on the horse."

"Stallion! Find a stallion this time. Ken was no more than a lame pony with one ball." Oh, that oyster-loving drunk chick was a piece of work. Mark was itching to get a peek at her.

"He had testicular cancer." Her voice was quiet and, although not meek, she definitely didn't sound as enthusiastic or keen on being there as the rest of them.

2

She sounded tired, sad.

"Okay, so he's a half-gelded lame pony. Whatever. Ditch the kiddie saddle and find a stallion you can bareback."

"Can we ditch the equestrian references please? They're creeping me out," Tori said with a groan.

"Look, Tori ..." Oh good, this friend sounded significantly less drunk and far more on the level. "We know Ken did a number on you."

"I filed for separation. I'm the one who called it quits."

"And rightfully so. You worked three jobs to put that bastard through dental school. He promised you once he finished, he'd put you through grad school, only instead he cheated on you with some little hoochie and left you high and dry."

"Yeah ..."

"Yeah?"

"But ..."

But what? Mark fought the urge to spin around. His instinct to protect overwhelmed him. Who on earth did that to a person? To their wife no less? He hadn't even met this woman, and yet the desire to find her ex and give the bastard a real piece of his mind was damn near all-consuming.

"But ... he was my husband. We took vows. For better or worse."

"Yeah, but Ken was beyond *worse*. Ken was despicable. And the shit he pulled is downright unforgivable. You did nothing wrong. Don't beat yourself up, and celebrate instead."

"That's right!" Oh shit, not the drunk friend again. "To divorce!" This cheer again?

Glasses clinked again, and more women cheered.

Call it stupidity, curiosity, and definitely the rye in his system, but before he knew what he was doing, Mark was up and out of his seat. Holy shit, there were more of them than he thought. A quick count said at least six women sat around the table.

He cleared his throat. "Excuse me, ladies, but I couldn't help overhearing—"

"Couldn't help?" The obnoxious one cut him off.

"Shut up, Mercedes, and let the handsome man speak," another woman scolded, slapping *Mercedes* on the shoulder. "Go on ... you were saying?" She flashed Mark a bright white smile, and heavily lashed brown eyes blinked at him.

Fighting not to roll his eyes, Mark offered the women a big smile instead. "Thank you. Yes, well, I was sitting right behind you and couldn't help but overhear that you're celebrating a divorce."

"That's right," Mercedes said with a nod, tossing her poker-straight blonde hair behind her with the kind of attitude you would expect from a moody teenager. "Tori here just separated from Ken, King of the Asswipes, and we are cel-e-brating!" She pointed to the cringing brunette in the corner with bright blue eyes and the color of absolute embarrassment staining her high cheekbones.

"Well, I'd like to offer to buy your table a round of drinks," Mark went on. "I'm no stranger to an ugly separation and divorce and being hurt, and I wish I'd had a group of friends to rally around me like this when it all went down."

Tori's eyes pinned on him. Jesus, she was a stunner. It didn't even look like she was trying, and the woman had the girl-next-door look down pat. Big pouty lips, long feathered lashes and, when she finally bestowed him with a smile, although small and demure, it stole his breath clear from his lungs.

"Ah, fuck. I'll cover your tab for the night. Drinks are on me." Well that came out before he could stop himself. Had the woman in the corner really put that much of a spell on him?

"Wow! Thanks, dude," Mercedes whooped, her light gray-blue eyes sparkling under the muted pot lights above the booth. "I may have judged you a bit too harshly. Thought you were coming over to tell us to be quiet."

"You ... uh ... you want to join us?" another woman offered.

"Mark. Just call me Mark."

"Care to join us for a moment, Mark?" She scooted over. "After all, it's the least we can do since you're covering our tab."

"And what a tab," Mercedes chimed in.

Mark wasn't sure he liked this woman. How did sweet little Tori know this woman? Were they BFFs? He certainly hoped not.

*How do you know she's sweet little Tori? She hasn't said a word to you.*

Yeah, but that dreamy pout and those big wide doll eyes said a lot.

Mark sat down next to the woman who offered him a seat, but his gaze remained fixed on Tori.

The woman he was sitting next to tapped him on the shoulder. "I have to use the ladies' room. Do you mind?" The club music was pumping, unlike a moment ago where it'd been low enough for him to overhear their booth, so they all had to kind of yell at each other. The new DJ liked it loud.

Just as quickly as he'd sat down, he was back standing up, letting three women (because women never went to the restroom alone) vacate the booth. Thankfully, one of those women was Mercedes.

"I'm going to order us another round on my way to the loo," Mercedes hollered, donning a fake British accent.

That left two more quiet girls on their phones and Tori in the booth. And of course, Mark.

Tori caught his eye. "Thank you."

He took his opening and scooted across the bench seat, leaning in next to her ear so he didn't have to yell. "You're welcome."

"So you're separated too?"

He nodded. "Yeah, divorced. Coming up on a year."

"I'm sorry."

"Yeah, me too. But it's for the best. So I overheard that you put your ex through school only for him to cheat on you with his colleague? Did you get to attend school at all?"

Her big sapphire orbs went wide, and with a single nod, she reached for her drink and finished it. "Yep and nope. All I have is my undergrad. He screwed me over for grad school. The prick."

"Wow. I'm really sorry."

She stifled a belch. "Thanks."

"What were you going to go to school for?"

She glanced at him out of the corner of her eye. "What's your angle here, dude?"

Oh, she had some spunk to her. He liked that.

Holding up his hands in surrender, he shook his head, hoping the look on his face was convincingly innocent. "Nothing. I swear. I was supposed to meet a friend here tonight, but he got called away last minute, so I decided to sit and finish my drink. That's when I overheard your party. To be fair, your friend Mercedes isn't exactly quiet."

Tori rolled her eyes. "We're not that close. She went to college with my younger sister. She's more Iz's friend than mine. And yes, she's extremely loud." She nibbled on her bottom lip for a moment, then spun to face him dead on. Something almost akin to panic graced her beautiful face. "But she's got a big heart. I don't *dislike* her. She showed up on my doorstep with wine, cheese and chocolate the moment I let the breakup cat out of its piss- and fur-filled bag."

Mark chuckled. "As long as her heart is big, I suppose."

"It is big ..." She glanced at the women across the table who were engrossed in their phones. "But so is her mouth. Sorry if she offended you at all."

"Takes a lot to offend me. Don't worry. She's been drinking. I'll give her a bye." His eyes ran over her body. She was wearing a black dress with a deep V that cut down past her cleavage. She wasn't big-chested, which was probably why she could pull off such a dress. She wore no jewelry, and her makeup was minimal. Like a sexy version of the girl next door. Not quite demure, but pure and perfect with just a touch of spice, a touch of dirty.

"Ya done?" she asked, clearing her throat.

Mark's eyes snapped up to her face. "Done what?"

"Checking me out?"

He also didn't embarrass easily. "Yep."

She scoffed and shook her head with a small smile. "I hope you also managed to overhear that I am in no position and have zero interest in *finding a stallion I can ride bareback* at the moment. I'm taking some time for *me*. I need to figure out my life. Figure out work and school."

"Right. I *did* hear that. Sorry, you're very beautiful, but I won't make a move. I promise. I get that things are still raw after your separation. It's never easy. Our hearts aren't made of rubber. They don't bounce back easily."

A small smile drew up the corner of her mouth. "Nice analogy."

"I've been known to come out with some good ones from time to time."

Eyes as crystal blue as Lake Louise glimmered back at him. Even under the weird lights at the club, he could tell they were vibrant and full of life. "I appreciate your understanding. Thank you."

He smiled. They were back in a good place. Excellent. "So, what do you do for work? What are you hoping to go to grad school for?

"Wow, you really were eavesdropping."

"Your friend ..."

She nodded. "Right. Mercedes. She's volume-challenged."

"So? What do you do for work?"

"Well ... I *used* to wait tables down at The Sunspear Bar and Grill three nights a week. I was also a dog walker three days a week, a cat sitter when needed, and I worked with children on the autism spectrum as an intervention therapist and educational assistant. I have my bachelor's degree in child and youth care, with a special focus on children with special needs and learning disabilities."

Mark nearly spat his rye out but managed to swallow it all down, causing his esophagus to spasm in the process.

Had she noticed?

The look she gave him said she did.

"You okay there, Mark?"

"Yeah, sorry. It's just, well ... I may have a job for you."

One eyebrow slowly slid up her forehead in skepticism. "Yeah?"

The woman was clearly jaded when it came to men, and she'd told him loud and clear that she wasn't interested in anything remotely resembling a relationship or otherwise. He needed to play this one cool. If she thought for one minute that he was only offering her the job to hit on her, she'd be out the door.

His mother, bless her flower-child soul, would call this fate.

Mark needed someone exactly like Tori in his life. And here she was.

"And what kind of a *job* would that be?" Her gaze slid down his body and landed on the crotch of his dress pants.

Wow, she was a ball-buster.

"Not *for* me. I just know of a job. A friend of mine is looking for an intervention therapist for his son. His son is on the spectrum, and they just lost his therapist a little while ago."

Her eyes perked up, and the disbelief faded from her face, though not entirely. "A *friend* of yours, huh? And what does this *friend* do?"

"He's a doctor. He's also divorced, like me. It's just him and his little boy, Gabe. Cute kid, crazy smart."

"How old?"

"Thirty-eight."

Her lip twitched into a sort of smile. "I mean Gabe. How old is Gabe?" She rolled those gorgeous blue eyes and shook her head. "Yes, how old is the dad? Good lord."

Mark chuckled. "Gabe is five. He just started kindergarten in September."

She nodded. "And your friend, what's his name?"

Mark swallowed. "Uh ... Chris. Dr. Chris Herron."

"Chris Herron?"

"Yeah."

"Oookay, let's say I'm interested. How would I go about applying with this *Dr. Herron?*"

"I can set it up. I can give you his phone number. That way you don't have to give me yours. And you can text him. I will let him know that I found someone who might be interested in the behavior interventionist job, and she'll be contacting him."

"You think texting is professional enough?"

Mark's head bobbed in agreement while the hair on the back of his neck prickled as the little white lie he'd started to spin slowly began to take on a life of its own. "Oh yeah, totally. He's a busy guy. Can't always answer the phone, but always has it on him to text."

"If you say so." She pulled out her phone. "Okay, give me his number."

"Ooooh, you guys swapping digits for a late-night booty call?" Mercedes clucked as she and the rest of the girls joined them back at the table. They had a tray of drinks with them, and soon everyone was downing doubles, all thanks to Mark.

"No, we're not," Tori said blandly. "He thinks he might know of a job opportunity for me, and I'm just getting the information."

Mercedes's blood-red-painted lips dipped into a pout for half a second. "Let's do some shots!"

Tori glanced at Mark. Holy hell, was the man gorgeous.

She'd sworn off men for the foreseeable future, but if there was ever a man to bring her back from the dark depths of sad divorcee-hood, it would be this guy. Because, boy oh boy, was he going to spur on some dirty dreams tonight. Probably for all the women. Including the married ones.

"I'm sorry," she muttered.

His chuckle made the blood run hot through her veins and fire flicker in her core. "I brought it on myself. I'm the one who interrupted ladies' night."

"This party wasn't my idea," she said, wincing from her strong drink. Holy hell, had Mercedes ordered triples? She was going to bankrupt him.

"Nothing wrong with blowing off a little steam or celebrating." His green eyes reminded her of the lush hills of Scotland. She'd always wanted to visit. And the way they bored into her made every muscle inside her body clench with need, particularly the muscles between her legs.

"Is that what you're doing? Blowing off steam?"

Thankfully, Mercedes hadn't been a complete drunken nut and had been kind enough to order Mark another drink as well. He tipped back the lowball with ice and took a sip. "I was supposed to meet a friend. He's going through some stuff and needed an ear to bend. But his daughter fell sick, so he had to cancel."

"I hope she's okay."

"I think so, just a cold. It's that time of year."

Mark checked his watch. And what an expensive watch it was. He was well dressed too. Nice dark, purple, long-sleeve, button-up dress shirt, black pants, and he had Tori's favorite accessory of all, scruff. Ken had always preferred to go clean-shaven. He said it itched less under the surgical mask when he was working in the dental office. But Mark had a nice healthy coat of dark whiskers dressing up his strong jaw. They were the perfect length too. Not too long, not too short. Just the right length to cause some whisker burn during a long makeout session.

He ran his hands through his dark hair, then yawned. "I think I should get going. It's getting late, and I don't want to intrude on ladies' night any longer." He made to get up to leave.

The other women in her group had decided they'd prefer to stand. A couple were entertaining male interest, giggling and swooning, while some were glued to their phones, texting with their boyfriends and husbands.

"Going so soon?" Suddenly Mercedes was right there, her hand on Mark's bicep, squeezing. "The party is just getting started ... thanks to you."

Mark gently shook her off and grabbed his leather jacket from the seat. "I'm afraid I must. But it was lovely meeting you ladies." His eyes found Tori.

"Particularly you, Tori. I hope you contact Dr. Herron and things with the new job work out."

Everything girly in Tori tingled. "Thanks. Me too."

As much as she swore she'd sworn off men, a big part of her didn't want to see him go. Didn't want the night, or their conversation, to end.

Should she give him her number?

She was about to say something when he leaned back over, his mouth falling next to her ear. Was he going to kiss her? She inhaled his scent. Holy mother. What was that cologne? The man smelled incredible. Like fresh air and man. All man. All sexy man with impeccable taste and the perfect amount of scruff.

But he didn't kiss her. Instead he whispered, "It gets better. Right now, I know it hurts. Right now, you hate men. Possibly even the world. But one day you'll wake up and realize you're so much better off. It does get better." Then he tucked a strand of hair behind her ear, pulled away, winked, and was gone.

"Wow!" Mercedes said, letting out a whistle, though Tori couldn't see her. Her eyes had fluttered shut the moment Mark tucked her hair. "I'm pretty sure I just had a mini orgasm."

Yeah, forget a mini orgasm. Tori was pretty sure she was in love.

# Chapter 2

♥

"Full house," Mark murmured, turning his cards over.

"Straight," Zak muttered, shaking his shaggy red head and finishing his beer.

"Ah ha!" Liam, the club founder and owner of the house, turned his cards over. "Royal flush. Read 'em and weep, suckahs!" His dark chocolate eyes gleamed with triumph as he began scooping all the poker chips from the center of the table toward himself.

Adam sat down with a new bowl of potato chips. "What'd I miss?"

"Just our host fleecing the shit out of us ... again," Zak, Adam's younger brother, grumbled, getting up from the table. "I guess the house always wins." He shook his head. "I need another beer. Anybody else?"

There were grunts and nods around the table.

"Yeah, because the high-powered divorce lawyer who makes six figures a year needs our money," chided Scott, Liam's younger brother, who'd been the first to fold.

"Hey, it isn't about need—it's about winning. All's fair in the game of poker." Liam grinned, reminding Mark of the Joker from Batman, with his wide and devious smile. "Besides, I'm not the only one bringing in six figures." He nodded at Mark. "Ol' Marky Mark isn't going to notice a dent in his pocketbook."

Mark rolled his eyes. He loved Saturday night poker. It was a place where he could be himself but also find support and camaraderie, since they were all single fathers.

Liam Dixon, host and club founder, was a divorce lawyer.

Although it was usually a big no-no to fraternize with clients, Liam had found a loophole and once he'd finished with their case, he became their friend. He brought the men he'd represented in court into his club. Men who he knew needed help navigating the messy seas of separation and custody, alimony and child support. And before any of them knew it, they were The Single Dads of Seattle and played poker every Saturday night.

Emmett sat down next to Mark. He'd folded early too and had been in the other room on the phone. His daughter, Josie, was with her mother but didn't want to be and kept calling Emmett, asking him to come pick her up.

"JoJo okay?" Mark asked Emmett, thanking Adam for his beer with a nod.

Emmett nodded. Mark wasn't convinced though. There was frustration in Emmet's amber eyes. It was taking everything he had in him not to jump up from the table and race to his daughter's rescue. "Tiffany has started dating and, against my wishes, introduced JoJo to Huntley, her new boyfriend. JoJo isn't happy, doesn't want anything to do with him, doesn't want to be there for dinner with him, wants him out of the house."

Mark frowned. Poor Josie.

Scott grabbed a handful of potato chips. "How long have you guys been separated?"

"Divorced," Liam chimed in. "That shit was final over a month ago, hence why you're here. You're no longer my client. Just my friend." He was all smiles.

Emmett made a face that had Mark wondering if his friend might be constipated. "Separated for over a year. But yeah, the divorce was final in November."

"And how long has she been seeing Huntley? Jesus, what kind of a name is that?" Mark asked.

"Right? That's what you name a dog." Emmett grabbed a bunch of pretzels from the bowl next to his elbow.

"It *is* the name of a dog. It's the dog from *Curious George*," Scott cut in.

Mark made a gesture that said "right!"

"It's actually *Hundley*, with a *d*," Adam corrected. "Mira loves *Curious George*. Hundley is her favorite."

"I love *Curious George*, too," Zak added. "Always up to so much mischief, but in the end, he saves the day."

Mark rolled his eyes. "Kind of like you?"

Zak's eyebrows bobbed up and down. "I definitely like to *monkey* around."

Emmett made a noise in his throat. "Anyway, she told me she's been seeing him for six months, which was our agreement. We're not allowed to introduce our kid to any new *partner* until the six-month mark. But even then, it should be done delicately. This divorce has been hard on JoJo." He shoved the pretzels in his mouth.

Mark fiddled with the label on his beer bottle. "Is JoJo at least feeling better?"

Emmett nodded, still chewing. He had to shove the food into the side of his cheek to talk. "Sorry I had to cancel last night."

Mark grabbed all the loose cards from the table and began to mindlessly shuffle them. "No worries."

"Did you just head home?"

He shook his head. "No. Finished my drink, then ended up spending over a thousand dollars on drinks for a table full of chicks celebrating their friend's separation."

All the guys around the table stopped talking, drinking, and chewing.

"You did what?" Zak asked. His divorce had been particularly nasty and was still quite fresh. Much like Tori, he'd sworn off women for a while and was concentrating on expanding his business. He owned three gyms in the Seattle area and was hoping to branch out to another two in the next two years.

Mark lifted a shoulder, continuing to shuffle. It was easier to keep his hands busy. "I overheard the party and felt sorry for her. Her husband made her put her dreams on hold and put him through school, only to cheat on her and leave her the moment he graduated. She worked three jobs to put him through school. Now she has no money to go to school herself."

"Who's representing her?" Liam asked.

Mark shook his head and snorted a laugh. "I have no clue."

"Who's representing him?"

"Again, no clue. I didn't ask that. But I did go over and offer to buy them a round."

"And that was a thousand clams?" Emmett asked.

"I kind of offered to cover their tab."

"Dude." Liam clucked his tongue. "That chick better have been a fucking ten or eleven for you to dole out that kind of money."

"She was ... *is*."

"You at least get her number?"

He shook his head. "No. She's sworn off men after the nightmare her ex put her through."

Zak made a rude noise in his throat. "Been there. I have no desire to date for a very long time."

"Just do what I do," Liam started, pointing at Mark to start dealing again for the next round. "Find a hot chick who's good in the sack and doesn't want anything serious, and bang her."

"You still sleeping with Richelle?" Scott asked him.

"She comes over every Wednesday night when Jordie is with Cidrah and we bang until the cows come home. She doesn't even stay the night."

"And she's cool with that?" Mark asked.

"She proposed it. Neither one of us wants anything serious, or to get the kids involved. Too fucking messy. We've seen the torture that kids can go through during divorce."

"Ain't that the truth," Zak murmured, picking his cards up off the table to look at them.

"It's how we met. She was on one side, and I was on the other, and we watched

15

as our clients used their children like pawns and bartering chips to get what they wanted. Fucking disgusting."

"Cidrah tried that with you," his brother said, shaking his head.

"She fucking *tried*."

"Good thing you're the best in the biz." Mark snickered.

"And you charge like you're fucking Beyoncé giving a private show," Emmett told Liam.

Liam's grin was wide, and he bobbed his eyebrows up and down playfully. "Don't I *deserve* my Audi for getting you shared custody of Josie? Plus, you're paying *half* the alimony Tiff was demanding."

Emmett snorted and rubbed the back of his neck. "Yeah ..." He glanced around at all the other men. "She wanted over six grand a month."

Adam nearly choked on his potato chips. "Six fucking grand? Not including child support?"

Emmett shook his head. "Not including child support."

Mark knew all this already, as he and Emmett were close. The men were all okay talking about their cases. This was their safe space. A place they came to bitch, moan, commiserate and speak freely. Ordinarily, Liam wouldn't have been able to mutter a word about a client's case, but things were different in the club. These men were family; these men had each other's backs. Nothing was off the table for discussion. Nothing was off limits.

"But Tiff is a fucking dermatologist," Adam said. "She makes good coin. What made her think she's entitled to so much?"

Emmett shook his head. "No clue."

"Greed," Liam interjected. "But the fact that she *is* a doctor and makes good money and also that JoJo is in kindergarten now, so Tiff can work more, brought Emmett's alimony *way* down."

Adam nodded. "That's good."

"Not everyone's divorce can be as amicable as yours," Liam replied.

Adam made a face that said he disagreed with Liam but wasn't up for a fight.

Adam's divorce may have been amicable, but it still wasn't easy.

"Tiff said that because she didn't get the alimony she asked for, she's going to introduce JoJo to *Huntley* however she wants. It's her retaliation," Emmett said, clearly distraught about the whole thing. "I know we agreed on six months, and Tiff is abiding by that. But it just feels like she's thrown Huntley into JoJo's face. He's sleeping over, has dinner with them all the time. He's trying to be JoJo's best friend, and she's not having any of it. She calls him a turd."

All the men around the table snickered, some of them commenting on how much they liked little Josie.

Like Mark, Emmett was a doctor at the hospital. But unlike Mark, who was a radiologist and could do a lot of work from home, Emmett was an ER and trauma surgeon and kept ungodly hours. He had to fight tooth and nail to get shared custody, because Tiff, who was a dermatologist and worked at a private practice from nine until two every day, said his hours didn't offer stability and structure to Josie. Liam had taken Tiff to town on that allegation, and luckily the arbitrator had sided with Emmett and awarded him equal time and rights to his daughter.

"Let's get back to the chick at the bar Mark *didn't* take home." Liam nodded at Mark, his dark blond hair falling down just slightly over his brown eyes. "So, what was so special about her for you to drop a grand on her and her friends?"

Mark was smiling. He'd been smiling a lot lately, every time he thought of Tori and that sexy dress with the deep V that would have gotten her kicked out of church. She had to be using some kind of double-sided tape to keep that thing in place. No way was it just staying put and not offering a nip slip without some kind of arts and crafts sorcery.

Liam clucked his tongue. "Look at him. It's like he's in a fucking trance."

Mark rolled his eyes at Liam and placed his bet. "I dunno. There was just something about her. We talked a bit …" He glanced down at his cards lying face down. "And then I offered her a job working with Gabe."

"You what?" Emmett was the one whose voice was the loudest, for obvious reasons. He and Mark were the closest. Mark had actually referred Emmett to Liam and his law firm for representation. They'd each witnessed the devastation their divorces had on the kids. Emmett was one of the few people Gabe trusted, besides family, and who Gabe was okay being left alone with. And his daughter, Josie, was the sweetest, most patient child in the world when it came to Gabe. She treated him like an ordinary kid. Played and spoke to him as if he were neurotypical and just another buddy at the playground. Even though Emmett and Mark worked together and saw each other most Saturdays for poker, whenever they could, they got together with the kids. Had dinner together, went on outings to the zoo and science center. It was just easier with two parents. Easier with someone who understood.

Mark took a sip of his beer, letting the cool San Camanez Island wheat ale slide down his throat. "It's not like she's not qualified. She works with children on the spectrum already and has a degree in child and youth care."

"Is that what you heard? Or is that what you *wanted* to hear, and your dick was too busy thinking of ways to get her out of her dress and into the back of your Beamer?" Scott asked, his slightly crooked nose wrinkling just so with his grin and looking even more crooked.

He said he'd broken it like four times in high school while playing football. Mark figured it was his smart mouth that had earned him a couple of breaks. Both the Dixon brothers had smart mouths and were known to speak their mind and piss people off with their lack of filter. Liam more than Scott, but neither of them was the most diplomatic of people.

"Have you done a criminal record check? Called her references? Why does she need a job? Was she fired from her last one?" Emmett continued.

Mark's gut twisted. No, but he was sure she would come back squeaky clean and with glowing references, he just knew it. At least he hoped he knew it. His friend seemed really perturbed by all of this. It both pissed Mark off and made him happy that Emmett was so protective of Gabe.

"When's she coming to meet Gabe?" Adam asked, his green eyes seeming to almost glow. His daughter, Mira, was another sweetheart who was so kind to Gabe.

"She hasn't texted Dr. *Christopher* Herron yet," Mark said, knowing that his deception was going to land him in seriously hot water with the sexy little Tori.

All the men cocked their heads in curiosity, but it was Adam who spoke. "What do you mean?"

"She doesn't know that it's me. I said I had a *friend* whose child needed therapy. I was afraid she'd think I was coming on to her."

Groans echoed around the card table. Mark knew what he'd done was stupid, but at the time he couldn't think straight. He'd had a few drinks, and Tori's smile, and those sparkling blue eyes, were drawing the blood from his brain and pooling it elsewhere. He hadn't been attracted to anyone, dated, slept with, even flirted with a woman since Gabe's mother had left and the divorce was finalized. But Tori's sweet smile and determined spirit stirred something deep inside him. He needed to see her again, and even if it was in a professional manner, he was going to make it happen.

They were just coming off the Christmas holiday, and he'd taken three weeks off work to be with Gabe. Friday night his mother had come over once Gabe was in bed so Mark could duck out and have a drink with Emmett. That was his first time out without Gabe in almost a month.

"What are you going to do when she figures out you lied to her? Which will happen the second she sees you answer the door?" Emmett asked. "You think she'll work for a liar? She's definitely going to think all you want is to get into her pants."

Liam shrugged. "Maybe that's exactly what he needs."

Emmett glared at Liam. "What he *needs* is to find someone for Gabe ... and the first interview should not be at a bar when you're ..."

"When I'm what?" Mark rounded on his friend. His hackles were rising. He knew what he'd done was dumb, but he was desperate to see her again. And, to be fair, when she said what she did for work, he'd jumped on it. He needed somebody for Gabe, and maybe this was the fates finally working in his favor.

Emmett lifted one shoulder and took a swig of his beer, wiping the back of his wrist over his lips. "I was going to say drunk."

"I wasn't fucking drunk. I'd had a couple doubles in the span of an hour or so. You know it takes way more than that for me to even get a buzz."

The other men were quiet around the table. Mark fought the urge to push himself away and head home. But this was part of poker night. Air grievances, talk shit out. Liam had once suggested setting up a sparring ring in his basement so they could kick the shit out of each other and let out some of their aggression, but nobody really wanted to get all sweaty and risk breaking their nose or getting a black eye. Most of them worked with the public.

"I'm just looking out for Gabe," Emmett said, his voice dropping a few octaves. He could tell he'd hit a nerve with Mark.

"I appreciate that. But I am too. I won't fuck this up. For me, Tori or Gabe."

Several heads shook around the table, but of course, it was Emmett who spoke up. "I hope so, dude. For all your sakes. Otherwise, you're out a grand, up shit creek without waders on with Gabe and a new therapist, and probably headed for a restraining order."

Mark flipped up his new card.

Full house.

His mouth tipped up into a small grin. "I think things are finally starting to go my way, boys. I bet you she'll text by tomorrow."

"And I'll represent you when it all goes south," Liam added. He elbowed his brother. "I should start handing out punch cards. Five divorces and the sixth one is free."

Scott glared at him. "Shut the fuck up."

# Chapter 3

"If you don't call me in an hour, I'm sending in the cavalry," Isobel said. The loud and jarring sound of her juggling her phone, keys and non-fat latte as she headed to her car caused Tori to hold her own phone away from her ear.

"And *who* is the cavalry?"

"Me and Mercedes. And the cops, of course. Though my money is on Mercedes delivering a better can of whoop-ass than any Seattle cop."

Tori chuckled. "If Friday hadn't gone as well as it did, I'd be cursing you out for bailing and leaving me with Mercedes all night."

Her sister groaned into the phone. "I said I was sorry. I ended up getting a last-minute job. And Mercedes said you had a great night."

"It was better than I thought."

"She means well. She's just a big personality ... a big mouth."

"Uh, yeah."

"But when you need her, she's there. My first breakup, the guy who took my virginity, you remember him?"

"Wolf?"

"Fox."

"Whatever. He was a dog."

"True. But anyway, Mercedes was there. She brought ice cream and movies, magazines and pizza. She really is a great friend, as drunk and obnoxious as she can get."

Tori glanced at the clock on the dash of her car. She'd been parked in front of Dr. Herron's house for fifteen minutes. She arrived early and called her sister. She needed somebody to know she was here. In case she never came out.

"Anyway, sis, I gotta jet. Thanks to you, I have a very busy dog walking business. The puppers won't walk themselves."

Tori turned off her car. "Yeah, me too. I'm heading in."

"Okay. Call me in an hour."

"Will do."

"Love you, Tor."

"You too, Iz."

Tori slammed her car door and faced the big, beautiful, white, suburban three-story house. Even though the driveway was clear, she chose to park on the street behind the cedar hedge that lined the front yard. How did Mark know Chris? Did they work together? Was Mark a doctor too? She'd asked him very little about himself, mostly because she didn't want to appear interested ... even though she kind of was.

Growling at herself and her inability to make up her mind about men and her life—and the fact that she overanalyzed, overthought and picked apart everything and everyone she met—she made her way up the driveway. It was wet from the rain. Because, well, it was Seattle and early January, so of course there was rain. Cold, wet, stick-to-your-bones-and-burrow-into-your-very-marrow rain. That was life on the west coast. It might not get negative double-digit cold, but when it did get cold, it sucked the big one.

Her hand came up and paused in front of the door. This was it. There was no turning back now. The job sounded great. And she needed a job. She needed a job desperately. She only hoped that Dr. Herron wasn't a weirdo. She could handle his kid. No matter where little Gabe fit on the autism spectrum, Tori would probably fall in love with him and find every day a new, rewarding challenge. But if the dad was a weirdo, she wasn't sure she could do it.

Taking a deep breath, she let her knuckles fall against the dark stained wood.

Twenty painful seconds.

They could have been hours for the amount of sweat on her palms and palpitations of her heart.

Twenty *long* agonizing seconds before the door swung open.

Wide, green eyes stared up at her.

"Uh ... hello. You must be Gabe."

The little boy with straw-colored hair and rosy cheeks simply blinked.

"Is your daddy home?"

More blinking, more staring. His eyes shifted so they were no longer looking at her, and he began to bounce on his toes.

"C-can I come in?"

He stepped out of the way, then began bouncing again.

Once inside the foyer, Tori crouched down so she was at eye level with Gabe. "Hi. I'm Tori. My favorite color is green, the same as your eyes. My favorite food is Tiger Tiger ice cream, and I think spiders are scary."

A small smile curled his mouth. His eyes blinked again but remained unfocused on her face. Mark hadn't said anything about Gabe, besides that he was on the spectrum. Was he verbal and just playing shy? Did he know any sign language?

She glanced around the big sixteen-foot-high foyer, hoping that Dr. Herron would show himself.

"So is your daddy around?"

Gabe reached for her hand, and with a strength she wouldn't have expected from such a slender kid, he hauled her into the depths of the house.

"Okay, then." She chuckled, following him as fast as she could, trying to peek into other rooms as she passed.

But they were too fast.

The whole house was a blur.

A big, beautiful, impeccably decorated, expensively decorated blur.

Gabe tugged her into a big room with an ocean theme painted on the wall and toys stacked in bins and scattered on a brightly colored foam puzzle-piece mat. He had a bunch of blocks organized in piles by color and what appeared to be the makings of a very impressive tower. Bringing her on to the mat, Gabe plopped down and, as if he hadn't just invited a total stranger into his inner sanctum, ignored her and went back to work on his tower.

This was weird.

Most bizarre job interview she'd ever been on, for sure.

Then again, it was smart. If she and Gabe clicked, did that mean she was a shoo-in? She still wanted to meet this Dr. Herron. Find out what Gabe's needs were, any allergies, triggers, preferences, etc.

Scanning the room, she searched for a nanny cam. Was she being watched?

Despite the ocean theme, there was a heck of a lot of red. All the toy bins were red, the child-size couch was red, the beanbag, the blankets.

"Is red your favorite color?" she asked.

Gabe looked up at her, almost as if seeing her for the first time.

"Is red your favorite color?"

His eyes crinkled in the corners, and he lifted up a red block, his smile growing wide.

"It is? Red is a great color. It's my dad's favorite color. He has a fancy sports car that's red." She looked around to see if she could find any Hot Wheels, but the closest she could find was a bright red wooden train caboose. But even if she had found a car, the little boy was no longer paying her any attention and was instead focusing intently on his tower. His very red tower. His fingers tapped each block as if counting them. Then suddenly he let out a wail, stood up and started hopping up and down, his head shaking and his arms flapping frantically.

The wailing grew louder and his frustration more intense.

Tori stood up and moved back, watching Gabe. If this was a fit, she needed to let it pass. The same for a tantrum. The intervention of a stranger would most likely just cause his behavior to escalate and he could hurt himself or her. But the longer she watched him, the more she realized he was upset about something specific. It wasn't a fit. And it wasn't a tantrum. He was looking for something. His eyes darted around the floor and room. His head thrashed to and fro as his hands stimmed, or flapped, and he bounced on his toes. Yips and wails slipped from his lips, along with sporadic grunts and groans.

He knelt back down next to his tower and tapped his fingers on each of the blocks. Counting them again. Then he sprang back up and began bouncing on his toes and thrashing his head.

He was missing a block.

All the blocks in his tower were red.

He was missing a red block.

Kneeling down again, she began to search. Gabe's hands flapped and he continued to bounce, an irritated growl-sounding hum rumbling through him.

"It's okay, buddy," she said softly, picking up toys and boxes in search of the missing block. "We'll find it. I'm sure it's around here somewhere. Couldn't have gone far." She picked up an overturned empty toy bin, and there it was. Lifting her gaze to the little boy, she softly said, "Hey, Gabe, look!"

But he was too busy, too frustrated, too caught up in his fear of the missing block to hear her. Poor kiddo.

She grabbed the block and, rather than stand up, she walked over to him on her knees so that they were on the same level. He was still bouncing on his toes and stimming his hands, but his eyes seemed to become a little more focused, and he watched her approach.

She held up the block in front of his face. "Look, buddy. Here it is."

Gabe's hands stopped. Followed by the bouncing. His gaze lasered in on the block, and his mouth stretched into a big smile. He grabbed the block and ran over to his tower.

Tori sat back on her heels and watched with satisfaction as he carefully placed the block on top, then, starting from the bottom just like before, began tapping each one—counting them.

Once he'd checked, then double-checked, that all the blocks were on the tower, Gabe spun around and raced toward her, flinging himself into her arms. His hug was tight, and he smelled like kids' watermelon-scented bubble bath. Not sure if she should hug him back, she withheld her embrace for a moment. But the kid wasn't letting go, and he smelled so good, felt so good in her arms, she relinquished her apprehension and hugged him back.

Kids' hugs were the absolute best.

They were so genuine, so tight, so truly amazing, that it was impossible not to feel good and full of hope and happiness after a good, long kid hug.

"Well, it seems as though you've won Gabe over," came a deep, masculine, and somewhat familiar voice from behind her.

Gabe's embrace paused, then he pulled away from her and ran toward the voice. Tori pivoted where she knelt only to find Mark from the bar standing in the doorway. He leaned sexily against the jamb, his hands casually stuffed into the pockets of his dark wash jeans and his dark hair a tousle of thick, luscious sexiness.

"Mark!" she exclaimed, pushing herself up to standing.

Grabbing Gabe's hand, he entered the playroom. "I'm sorry for the deception." He held out his other hand. "Dr. Mark *Christopher* Herron, and Gabe's dad. A pleasure to meet you ... again."

Before Tori could say anything, Gabe shook his grasp from his father's and instead reached for Tori's hand. He pulled her back over to the foam mats and encouraged her to sit. She did, and he plunked himself right in her lap, busying himself with taking down his red block tower and reorganizing it into a different tower.

Mark followed them deeper into the playroom and sat down in the

26

ketchup-red beanbag chair, watching her and Gabe intently.

Tori shook her head. This was all so overwhelming. Here she thought she was coming for a job interview with a Dr. Chris Herron, not Mr. Dirty Dreams from Friday night. And he wasn't just interviewing her for a job; he was offering her *the* job of a lifetime. A job that would help her toward her goal of becoming a behavioral consultant, a job working with a child with special needs. It was exactly what she wanted. Exactly what she needed.

She picked a piece of lint off Gabe's shoulder. "I'm sorry, but can you start from the beginning? I'm a little overwhelmed at the moment. Not to mention surprised."

And thanks to the fact that his smile was what dirty dreams were made of, and his eyes a wickedly wild and grassy green, she was not only overwhelmed but also slightly aroused. Should she push the child out of her lap?

Baseball!

Football!

Her gross uncle John eating super saucy chicken wings without a shirt on.

Yep! That did it.

That thought killed the lust.

That thought killed everything.

Mark smiled that sinfully yummy smile of his. She bet those lips tasted like vanilla cupcakes. "I apologize for not being entirely honest on Friday when I mentioned the job. I thought if you didn't know that it was me who needed the position filled, you'd be more likely to consider it and not think I was just coming on to you."

*Position filled.*

Shit. Her mind was back in the gutter.

Uncle John eating chicken wings without a shirt on sitting in a kiddie pool filled with Jell-O and humming the tune of "Barbie Girl."

*Phew.*

Okay, she was back in business.

"Gabe is a bit of a handful." He leaned forward and ruffled his son's hair when the little guy spun in Tori's lap at the mention of his name. "A wonderful handful, but a handful nonetheless. He doesn't do well with change and transition. He's a creature of habit."

Tori made a face. "Aren't we all?"

Mark chuckled. "You'll think you're a disorganized mess compared to Gabe. You should see his room. Everything is spotless and in its rightful place. We've determined that he functions best when he knows what's coming. Surprises are not his friend. He also doesn't do well with new people constantly introduced into his routine."

Tori's eyes went wide. Then how was he currently sitting in her lap, humming contently, when they'd only just met less than twenty minutes ago?

"I know. I'm as shocked as you are that he's taken to you so well and so quickly. This is a one-off. But it's also why I'm offering you the job without having even checked your references. Nobody has ever won my son over this fast before. He's never hugged a therapist, let alone climbed into their lap. I *will* check your references, but barring anything alarming, I'm still prepared to offer you the job."

She swallowed. All she'd done was locate the kid's missing red block, and suddenly she was his new best friend.

"Gabe goes to school five days a week. He's in a regular class setting with neurotypical children and generally does very well. However, funding has been cut, and he no longer gets the one-on-one support he needs. The educational assistant has been allotted to the *class* and not the student. Gabe *needs* one-on-one support. He's prone to tantrums, outbursts, and his social skills are not where they should be. He'll walk right up to a person in a restaurant and steal a fry off their plate if he's hungry, take a toy from a child at the park if he wants it. He needs the support of someone devoted solely to him."

Tori nodded. "I get that. It's a shame the funding was cut, though not surprising. I've heard that's happening a lot."

Mark's head bobbed, and he exhaled through his nose. "It is. It's frustrating. Add on top of it all that his last intervention therapist left with only three days' notice, needless to say, we've been struggling."

"Does he have a speech path? An occupational therapist?"

"He has both, plus a behavioural consultant."

"And he or she has programs done up specifically for him?"

"She does. They all do. He sees the speech path once a month, OT twice a month, and BC every six weeks."

"Okay."

"I need you to be here for him all day. Meaning, I want to hire you to be his support at school, as well as his support at home. I'll pay you for a full ten hours and double time for any overtime. He needs consistency and somebody he trusts." His eyes softened as he took in Gabe in Tori's lap. The child was happily stacking all the red blocks single file into the tallest tower he could manage. "And he seems to trust you."

Ten hours a day? What about school? She didn't want to be a nanny. She didn't want to be an intervention therapist for the rest of her life. She had big goals. Goals of becoming a behavioral consultant herself and opening up her own practice. Hiring all kinds of different therapists to help out children who needed it most. She couldn't give that all up now.

Ever since her first job as a babysitter at twelve years old, she'd fallen in love with children. And over the years, she'd done a lot of babysitting for family and neighbors, family friends and even for her dad's chiropractor and his family. She spent her summers nannying or as a camp counselor. But it was during her sophomore year in high school, when she was a camp counselor for a special-needs camp, that she found her true calling. In fact, it was one child in particular—Seth, a sweet little seven-year-old boy with Downs Syndrome and autism, who had helped her realize what she was meant to do with her life, who she was meant to work with.

Seth had taken such a shine to her that his parents had hired her to do respite work with him for eight hours every weekend. She'd worked with him right up until she graduated high school. Even now, his parents sent her updates on him and pictures.

She went to open her mouth, to protest his job proposal and see if she could negotiate, but Mark cut her off.

"Whatever you were making at your other jobs, I'll double it."

Tori's bottom lip damn near hit Gabe on top of the head.

"I also want to pay for your schooling."

What the hell?

"I've spoken with Gabe's behavioral consultant, and she is willing to consider you for a practicum position. You'd have to apply with her on your own merits, but she *is* currently accepting new practicum students. Apparently, you can do the majority of your schooling by distance, which would allow you to be with Gabe during the day."

"Y-you want to pay for my schooling? Dr. Herron, I can't accept such a generous offer."

"Please, call me Mark. Again, I apologize for being dishonest on Friday. I should have been up front that it was me who needed the therapist for my son."

Tori's mind was running a million miles a minute. "Fine, Mark. I appreciate your offer, but I can't allow you to pay for my schooling."

His dark brows narrowed in adorable confusion. "Why not? You want to go back to school, which I totally respect and encourage, but you can't afford it. I can. I need somebody like you to help me with my son. It's a win-win."

"But ... "

"Talk to Janice Sparks, Gabe's behavioral consultant, and look into the practicum she's offering. We can take it from there. But I don't want you to give up on your dreams because you simply can't afford them."

He was like her fairy godfather or something. Arriving just in the nick of time. When things couldn't be closer to rock bottom, he sprinkled fairy dust that smelled like scrumptious manly cologne and turned her rotting pumpkin of a world into a beautiful Ferrari of new hope.

That's how the story went, right?

Could the fairy godfather also be Prince Charming? Could he pull double duty?

"I'm going to call your references in the morning, but I would like for you to start as soon as you're able to. Do you need to give your other jobs notice?"

Had she even accepted the position?

He was just so persuasive, so charming, so ... dreamy. His voice, his eyes, the way his lips moved when the spoke had her mesmerized.

Oh shit.

Creepy Uncle John eating chicken wings without a shirt on, sitting in a kiddie pool full of Jell-O, humming "Barbie Girl" and showing off his long, fungus-covered toenails.

*There we go.*

She'd never be able to look at her Uncle John the same way again, but that didn't matter. He was finally being useful. And not just grossing the crap out of her family and annoying the shit out of her father.

"Tori?"

"Huh?" She closed her eyes and shook her head, visions of Uncle John, chicken wings and Mark's emerald eyes bouncing around behind her closed lids.

"You okay? I asked you when you could start."

Crap.

"Um, I just have my dog walking business right now, but my sister is actually doing it for me at the moment."

"What happened to the other jobs?"

She let out a sigh and picked up a red block next to her hip and mindlessly passed it Gabe. The little guy grinned up at her and happily stacked it on top of his tower. "After I found out Ken cheated on me, I started to spiral a bit. I couldn't get out of bed, and it wasn't fair to my jobs, so I quit them. The restaurant, the therapy company. I gave my dog-walking business to my sister."

He nodded, his eyes crinkling in the corners as his mouth twisted in an understanding half-smile. "I get that. Been through a nasty divorce myself."

"It takes a lot out of you."

"It certainly does."

"You're feeling better though, right?" Unease flashed behind his eyes.

She hoped her smile mitigated some of his concern. "I am, yeah. Wallowed in self-pity for a bit there, but I picked myself up by my bootstraps and am doing much better. I didn't mean to scare you there. Sorry."

His eyes fell back on his son. "Onward and upward, it's all any of us can do, right?"

"Sounds about right." She blew out a breath. "How did the divorce affect Gabe?" She knew that divorce could be rough on even neurotypical kids, having their routines and households turned upside down, but it could be even more difficult for children on the spectrum.

The thin, grim line of his mouth said it all. "It was hard on Gabe. He really struggled. A lot of new behaviors came out of it, and not all of them good."

"Makes sense. Is it tough, the back and forth between your house and his mother's house?"

Oh crap. She hadn't even asked if she was going to be required to work for Gabe's mother as well. How awkward would that be?

"She's not in the picture."

"She—"

Was she dead? Had they divorced and then she died? Had he killed his wife? *Way to jump to the most ludicrous conclusion. Yeesh!*

"She left. Signed over custody and everything. She's moved across the country. Found Gabe's diagnosis too much to deal with."

Her hand flew to her mouth, covering her gasp. "I'm so sorry."

His jaw tightened, and those beautiful eyes she was quickly finding herself getting lost in developed a harsh glint to them. "Don't be. We're in a good place now, me and Gabe. But my job is demanding, so that's why I need the help."

"What kind of a doctor are you? Do you not keep weird hours?"

"I'm a radiologist. And yes, sometimes I do. But I'm an attending, so my hours are flexible. I can also do a lot of work from home, and I do, once Gabe is in bed. It will typically be an 8 a.m. to 6 p.m. kind of day, but sometimes I may need you to stay later."

Before she knew what she was doing, Tori tilted down her neck and smelled the top of Gabe's head. Her eyes closed.

When she opened them again, Mark was watching her. Fire burned behind the intense green, and his nostrils flared. "Does Monday work for you?"

"Monday?"

"To start."

Wow! Here just yesterday she wasn't sure how she was going to afford groceries and school for the next few months, and now today she had a brand-new job, paying double what she'd made at her other jobs, and somebody was willing to pay for school.

"Do you think Gabe will be okay with me accompanying him to school?"

"Let's ask him." He slipped off the bean bag and knelt in front of his son. His knee touched Tori's, and a spark raced through her body. He placed a big, tanned hand on his son's shoulder. "Eyes on me, buddy." Gabe lifted his head, but Tori couldn't tell if he was looking at his father. Eye contact could be a challenge for children with Autism Spectrum Disorder, or ASD. Mark's other hand fell to the block in Gabe's hand. The little boy grunted his frustration and made to pull away, but Mark stopped him. "Eyes on me." Mark's smile melted Tori's insides. "Good. Do you want Tori to come to school with you?"

Gabe's head whipped around, and he stared at Tori. This time, the eye contact was undeniable. His smile was enormous, showing off all his pearly white teeth.

"Should she come to school with you? Maybe hang out with you at home after too?"

Gabe's head bobbed in a nod, then he flung his arms around her neck so hard she toppled over where she sat, taking them both down to the ground. All to the warm, melodic laughter of Mark "Dr. Dirty Dreams" Herron.

# Chapter 4

♥

"So, how'd the first day go?" Mark asked, wandering into his kitchen Monday night to find Gabe and Tori sitting at the table playing a matching game.

His kid looked happy.

Tori glanced up from their game, her smile making him trip over nothing but his attraction to her. "Pretty good."

"And school?" He sat down next to Gabe and ruffled his son's hair before pecking him on the forehead. Gabe didn't so much as glance his father's way. He was too engrossed in the Ninja Turtles matching game he loved so much.

Tori nodded, this time not bothering to look up at him. "There were a few tears when they abruptly canceled P.E. class because some of the overhead lighting had come down, and electricians were in there. But when we went outside for a quick run around the school and splashed in some puddles, he was all smiles again."

"That's it?"

Mark called the school after he knew Tori and Gabe had left for the day. He spoke with Gabe's teacher and asked for feedback on Tori and how she was with Gabe. You can never be too careful, and even though he had called all of Tori's references and received nothing but glowing praise from all her former employers, he wanted to know what Gabe's teacher thought of her. Mrs.

Samuelson had nothing but positive things to say, too. She even said that Tori spearheaded a game with the whole class that Gabe could easily participate in, and Gabe even won. Normally, Gabe didn't participate in many games because he wasn't verbal and so many of the activities involved verbal or sign-language communication. Gabe knew some signs, but he wasn't consistent with them, so it made communication tough.

According to Mrs. Samuelson, though, Gabe had been all smiles and participated with the other children without any incidents or frustrated outbursts.

He hadn't had a good day like this in a long time. Possibly ever.

Tori lifted her head and focused on his face, her lips twisted as if she was hiding something. "I hope you don't mind, but seeing as it was our first day and everything had gone so well, I stopped at the smoothie shack on the way home and we grabbed smoothies as a treat. I know you want us to come straight home from school, have a nutritious snack and then begin working on therapy programs. But ..." She shifted her gaze back to Gabe. "We had smoothies, drank them down on the dock and watched the boats, then came home. We've been working on therapy programs ever since."

Mark's heart constricted inside his chest. He loved that she was so interested in his son, so devoted to making sure Gabe enjoyed his day and adjusted well. He didn't care that they went for smoothies or that they went down to the dock. What he cared about was that his son had a smile on his face, had made it through the entire day at school and had eaten something. Those were Mark's goals for Gabe, and on day one, Tori had already surpassed them.

But the face he was making as he stared at them playing their game must have confused her, because with a tremulous voice, she brought him out of his thoughts. "I made sure to pack the smoothie with spinach and a scoop of protein powder. So it was actually pretty healthy. And I spent the weekend poring over the programs his behavioral consultant sent me, and I managed to implement a few on the dock. Obviously adapted to life skills rather than classroom, but he still did really well."

He smiled at her. "I'm not mad at all, Tori. You did amazing. He's never had a first day with a new therapist as successful as this. Keep doing what you're doing, and I don't think we'll have any issues."

Her bright blue eyes glimmered beneath the contemporary lights that hung over the big, natural-edge kitchen table. "He's a lot of fun."

Mark glanced down at his son. "That he is." With a groan, he pushed himself back up out of his seat. "He's also a picky eater, so I'm happy if you managed to get some veggies and protein into him. Dinner is always a struggle." He wandered over to the fridge and opened it. He'd debated picking something up on his way home, but his new year's resolution had been to cook more at home and not let laziness and fatigue interfere with him making his son a home-cooked meal. "What do you feel like for dinner, bud? Mac and cheese? Spaghetti? Grilled cheese and tomato soup? Mashed potatoes and chicken tenders?" Pretty much the four things he knew his son would eat.

He'd picked up a cookbook over Christmas that was all about slipping vegetables into food undetected, so that kids were none the wiser, but still getting the nutrition they needed. He'd managed to throw cauliflower into mashed potatoes, butternut squash into his mac and cheese, and spinach into his spaghetti. But Gabe was becoming wise to his deception, and meals were getting tough again.

"Dinner's actually already made," Tori said, her voice once again full of hesitation. "I hope you don't mind."

Mark spun around. "You made dinner?"

She shrugged, causing the wide neck of her striped gray T-shirt to slip off and expose one shoulder and a black bra strap. Mark had to stop himself from groaning.

"Gabe helped me. He wanted spaghetti, so we did it together. He's a great helper in the kitchen. Did all the stirring."

Gabe beamed next to her.

She cupped her mouth and brought her voice down. "I set the tablet up for ten minutes and let him watch a show so that I could puree some spinach, peppers, carrots and broccoli into the sauce without him noticing."

Mark shook his head in disbelief. "Has he eaten it?" As much as he loved the fact that dinner was already made and he didn't have to wait with a growling gut to eat and then fight his child to eat, he also really enjoyed dinner time with Gabe. It was where they connected, where they bonded. Even before Cheyenne had left, family dinner time had been sacred.

She shook her head. "I asked him if he was hungry and wanted to eat before you got home or if he was okay to wait. He said he was okay to wait."

"How did he tell you that?"

She made the American sign language sign for *wait*. "He told me."

"You speak ASL?"

"A fair bit. Not fluent, but enough to get by. We've been signing a lot today. He's very communicative."

"He is?"

Her expression was curious as she stood up and made her way over to the stove where two pots sat. She turned both elements on. "Does he not sign with you?"

"Not consistently." Mark wandered back over to sit next to Gabe. It felt weird letting her take over the kitchen and dinner, but she didn't seem to mind. If anything, she appeared right at home in his kitchen. Very comfortable.

She shrugged before reaching into the cupboard and bringing out two plates. "Odd. I haven't had any communication issues with him today."

"He must really like you."

She grinned back at him as she opened up the cutlery drawer. "I hope so, because I really like him."

"Has he tried the sauce?" Mark asked, in awe of this woman and how in one day she'd already managed so much with his son. If Gabe had tried the sauce and liked it, Mark was ready to fall at Tori's knees and bow in reverence.

She shook her head. "Not yet. But fingers crossed."

His gaze fell to the two plates she had waiting, and he got up again and carefully traversed the small space behind her, mindful not to accidentally touch her. Her presence in his house alone muddled his brain; accidentally touching her would probably send him over the edge. But he was close enough to smell her. Turning his face to the cupboard, he shut his eyes and inhaled. Fuck, she smelled good. He couldn't tell what it was, but it smelled floral and feminine and it suited her.

He grabbed another plate and put it down next to the other two.

She glanced up at him with confusion.

"May as well join us, seeing as you made it."

Tori shook her head and went to grab the plate, but he stopped her. This time their hands touched and a charge zapped him. It ran straight from her soft, delicate fingers through his arm to his heart, only to settle down somewhere between his legs.

"I don't want to impose or intrude," she said, quickly tugging her hand out from under his. "I only made supper because it was getting late and I figured it was a good way to work on counting and fine motor skills. He counted all the spaghetti noodles before I put them in the pot, picking up each one with his fingers."

That was a brilliant idea. Why hadn't he thought of that? He was always looking for more ways to get Gabe involved in day-to-day activities and help out around the house, as well as implement his programs into their daily lives.

Now she had to stay.

Knowing what it would do to him and hoping she didn't get the wrong idea, even though all he had were wrong ideas when it came to Tori, he put his hand on her shoulder. "Please stay. Like you said, it was such a great day, we should all celebrate. And since you made it, you should really enjoy it too."

Her top tooth snagged her bottom lip. He wanted to bite that lip.

"Unless of course you have plans?"

Her gold-chain necklace was askew, and the small heart pendant sat in the hollow of her long, sexy neck. Her throat bobbed on a swallow, and she licked her lips.

Fuck, he still hadn't removed his hand from her shoulder. And it was the bare shoulder too. So his hand was actually on her silky, soft skin. On her bra strap.

"N-no plans," she stammered, licking her lips again. "I just don't want to intrude."

Reluctantly, he pulled his hand away. "No intrusion at all. We'd love to have you stay." He turned to Gabe. "Right, buddy?"

Gabe's smile was huge.

Tori wiped her mouth with her napkin and sat back in her chair, admiring the unruly way Mark's dark hair twirled down just over his ears and stuck up slightly near his forehead. It was roguish and wild, but it suited him. As did the close-trimmed beard that clung to his jaw.

He cracked an unexpected smile that emphasized his dark good looks. "Well, Miss Jones, I think you're a miracle worker. Look at that kid's plate."

Gabe was using his finger to mop up the last of the spaghetti sauce, having already devoured the pasta and garlic bread.

"I will admit I put a secret ingredient in there when he wasn't looking. Makes it irresistible to children."

Mark lifted his eyebrows, waiting.

"Crack."

His smile grew wider and sexier—if that was possible.

"Know a guy who sells it for cheap. Goes by the name of Slime, but his stuff is legit. He mainly peddles it out near Rosemont Elementary, hits up those parents. Makes a killing."

His warm chuckle, along with an appraising gaze rolled over her, made her want to wrap it around herself like a cashmere throw. "Well, give Slime my regards, because whatever can get my kid to eat his veggies, I am one hundred percent on board with. I'll write Gabe a script for methadone if it becomes a serious problem."

Tori tilted her head back and whooped out a laugh. She was glad he had such a great sense of humor. Ken would have looked at her like she was nuts. He never thought her dry and slightly dark sense of humor was funny.

"Do you have other recipes and tricks up your sleeve?" he asked, standing up and taking his plate, and then hers, to the dishwasher.

She thanked him and followed with the marinara bowl and garlic bread basket. "I have a few, yeah. Bought a cookbook on how to sneak veggies into meals for kids."

Mark stopped loading the dishwasher and instead opened up the cupboard above it, pulling a book down from a row full of cookbooks. "You mean this one?"

Tori chuckled. "That's the one. Though she typically just adds one or two veggies to each recipe. I say go big or go home and I add a bunch. Plus, I've modified some of her recipes and come up with a few of my own."

Mark shook his head and put the cookbook back. "I've made a few recipes from her book as well, but either I'm not making the recipe right, or Gabe is a super taster, because he still turns his nose up at the majority of them. He's gotten wise to my ploys."

She placed the leftover marinara sauce in a glass storage container, then put it in the fridge. "Well, I'd be happy to make a few more meals for him"—she turned to face him—"and you, if you'd like. I don't mind. It gives us something to do once I know he's too tired for programs."

"I can't ask you to make us dinner." She could tell by the tone of his deep voice that he really wanted her to cook for them, but he felt that it was asking too much.

She knew what it was like to come home after a long day of work, only to have to then whip up dinner. She'd work a ten- or twelve-hour day between her jobs, hoping and praying that Ken would have at least thought to pull something out of the freezer for dinner, only to come home and find him vegged out on the couch, "studied out" and waiting for her to make dinner. She understood that he was studying his butt off, but she was working her butt off and then was still expected to do all the cooking and cleaning.

Their marriage had never been equal, had never been fair.

"I know what it's like to be too tired to cook," she finally said. "I don't mind. If that's what you'd like. I mean, I *am* making Gabe dinner, and preparing his meals is part of my job description, no?"

"It is ..." he said hesitantly. His eyes fell on Gabe, who was sitting droopy-eyed at the table. The poor kid was nearly falling asleep on his plate. He'd been such a trooper all day, he had to be exhausted.

"I should get going," she said, sensing the sudden change in the atmosphere of the room. "Let you guys get back to your routine. I've interfered enough."

Mark's green eyes shot back up to her. "No. Just ..." He ran his hand through his hair, appearing almost flustered. "Just stay here for a moment. Let me run Gabe his bath and get him all set up. Then I'll come out and talk to you." His gaze intensified until it seemed he was pleading with her. "Please?"

She nodded, taking Gabe's plate away from him. It was so clean, she could almost put it back in the cabinet.

Mark grabbed a sleepy-eyed Gabe and hoisted him up onto his hip. "Come on, big guy. Let's get you in the bath so you can hit the hay. You've had such a big day, no wonder you're tired."

Gabe's eyes popped open wide, and he glanced back at Tori with trepidation, his bottom lip wobbling just a touch.

"It's okay," she said, giving him a big reassuring smile as she dried her hands on a dish towel. "I'll be back tomorrow, and we'll do it all again. You go with your dad and have a nice warm bath."

His eyes settled back into sleep mode, and he let his cheek rest on Mark's shoulder. But his hand flew out, and he signed a butchered one-handed version of "good night" to her just before they rounded the corner to the bathroom.

"'Night, buddy. Sweet dreams."

Unease swam through her as she sat at the kitchen table and thumbed through her phone, waiting for Mark to return. He seemed to be appreciative of everything she'd done so far. Their dinner banter and his laughter at her jokes seemed like a good sign. He'd invited her to stay and eat with them. Had something happened she wasn't aware of? Had she overstepped in some way? Was he displeased? Was he dismissing her? Why had he asked her to stay?

*Stop overthinking things!*

She'd already fallen head over heels for Gabe, so she couldn't imagine leaving him, and she also really needed this job. She needed to save up for the next few months so she could get her own place when her parents' friends returned from Arizona in the spring. A nice little nest egg would be very helpful for starting back out on her own. Plus, she'd been emailing back and forth with Janice Sparks all weekend, and the practicum position sounded amazing. She could work right alongside Janice, getting her practicum hours at the same time she was doing her schooling. She'd be a certified behavioral consultant in no time.

It was closing in on seven o'clock. Was she still on the clock?

She still had laundry to do and was going to start reading some of the online modules Janice had mentioned.

A text message from Ken popped up. She deleted it without reading it. That was the third one this week. He'd also sent two emails. She'd deleted those, too. She had nothing to say to him. If he wanted to speak to her, he could hire a lawyer and do it that way. She needed to save some money first so she could do the same.

Tori blew out a long, slow exhale. Fucking Ken, even when they were over, he was still causing her grief.

She heard Mark's footsteps coming down the hall and hastily switched off the screen of her phone, setting it down next to her arm.

He approached with the loose-limbed gait of a man in total control. A man who knew his worth and rarely ever heard the word *no*. "Little guy is out. He could hardly keep his eyes open during his bath and didn't last two pages of his favorite Harvey the Happy Puppy book. Whatever you did knocked him right out."

"It's the crack, I'm telling you."

The man could be a model for Crest, his smile was so perfect. "Must be. Maybe it's laced with tryptophan?"

"Wouldn't that be something? An upper and a downer all in one."

He sat down across from her at the table, stretching his corded neck side to side until it popped. Thickly muscled arms and shoulders strained the seams of a black T-shirt he must have changed into after putting Gabe down.

She simply waited. Waited and ogled. It was hard not to. The man was gorgeous.

Green eyes as vibrant as cut emeralds stared back at her. In all her life, she'd never met a man who was so inherently alpha male as Mark Herron. He was commanding, confident, intimidating and yet completely drool-worthy. He stirred something inside Tori she hadn't felt in ages. Had she ever felt it? She couldn't remember being this attracted, this primitively drawn to Ken.

Letting out an exhale that could only be from a long, hard day spent saving lives, he folded his big, capable hands in front of him on the table. She stared down at his hands, envisioning them wrapped around her waist, caressing her breasts, playing with her hair ...

"I want to thank you again," he started, snapping her out of her fantasy. "I know I went about hiring you in a rather unorthodox way, and I appreciate you giving us—me and Gabe—the chance. He seems positively smitten with you, so whatever you're doing, keep it up. His teacher was thoroughly impressed with you, too."

Had he called and spoken with Mrs. Samuelson? The glint in his eyes said he had. It also said he would always keep tabs on his child and that everything with Gabe, and with her career inside and outside the home, was transparent. And would remain as such.

He didn't bother to expand on that and simply continued. "I do want to offer to pay you more to cook dinner for us. There are no adequate words to express my gratitude for coming home to dinner already cooked. And the fact that Gabe ate it all ..." He blew out a breath. "I can't remember the last time he *licked* his plate clean."

"He's a great kid." It's all she could think of to say. His intense stare was flustering her.

"I'd also like you to stay and eat with us when you can. Give us a chance to get to know each other, and that way you're not forced to go home and delay your own meal. You're feeding us. The least we can do is feed you."

"That's not necessary—"

He cut her off. "I insist. When you can. If you have plans"—he paused—"or a *date*, you're more than welcome to leave when I get home. But don't feel like you *have* to leave if you don't have anything to get home to. It will give us a chance to discuss Gabe's day, his progress, his challenges and anything else."

Anything else ...

She couldn't keep eye contact with him any longer and let her gaze drop to the table. "Thank you. That's very kind."

The man had the ability to turn her to mush. One minute she was all confident and carefree, cracking jokes about crack, and then the next she could hardly sit still for the frenzy of horny butterflies going berserk in her belly.

The air in the room suddenly changed. It was thick and heady. Pheromones pinged and bounced off the ecru-colored walls.

"You're an excellent cook."

She glanced up at him beneath her lashes. "Thank you."

Why was she so nervous around him?

*Maybe because he's a thirty-eight-year old doctor who you'd love to* play *doctor with. Only he's also your boss, and you really need this job.*

She blew her bangs off her forehead, her eyes flicking to the clock on the stove.

Mark followed where she was looking. "I guess it's getting late. I won't keep you any longer." He stood up, and she followed suit, walking over to the small bench along the wall to retrieve her purse and bag.

In silence, they wandered to the foyer. He grabbed her coat off the coatrack, and she thought he was just going to hand it to her, but like a gentleman, he held it out, waiting for her to slip into it.

His knuckles grazed the side of her neck as she slid her arms into the jacket. A spark from his touch raced through her, causing her nipples to harden to tight points. She took a step forward, away from the heat of his body, the manly smell of him. Slowly, she spun around to face him, doing up the buttons on her pea coat, then freeing her hair at the nape of her neck.

All the while he simply watched her, not saying a word.

Was there tension? Was there something going on between them? Or was it all in her head? She couldn't tell. Was he always this intense? It was overwhelming.

She was stone-cold sober, and yet being around Mark made cotton cloud her brain and rattled her thoughts, as if she'd just put her head in a paint mixer.

He shoved his hands in the front pockets of his light, well-worn, sexy-as-fuck jeans and rocked back on his bare feet. "We'll see you tomorrow then."

She secured her purse over her shoulder and nodded. "Yes, tomorrow."

He opened the door for her. Like a gentleman. "Have a good night."

She swallowed past the hard lump in her throat and took a step forward, her body not wanting to leave the warmth of Mark's home. Not wanting to leave Mark. She stopped on the welcome mat outside. The eaves dripped from the light rain. It was dark outside, but the porch light made the yard glow, illuminating the fog. He leaned against the doorjamb, hands back in his pockets, legs crossed at the ankle.

Had she ever seen anything hotter in her life?

No.

"Good night, Tori. Sweet dreams."

Her chest rose and fell quicker than on any run she'd ever taken. "Yeah ... you too."

Then she headed to her car, drove to the drugstore and bought a twenty-four pack of double-A batteries. Her vibrator had no idea what was in store for it tonight.

# Chapter 5

♥

He could hear the screaming from inside the house the moment he turned off the ignition in his car. He knew that sound well.

Poor Gabe.

Poor Tori.

She had been with Gabe for almost a month now, and things were going fantastically. His kid had shown more progress in these past four weeks than he had in years. But today Tori texted him to let him know that Gabe was having a rougher day than usual. There was a substitute teacher at school, as Mrs. Samuelson was sick, and Gabe did not like the change. He'd refused to eat his snack or lunch, took a swing at one of his classmates and was, according to Tori, "struggling" all day. Mark knew she was sugar-coating it, though. He'd called the principal a few hours ago and had a good chat with her. The substitute teacher—poor thing—had been traumatized by Gabe's outbursts, tantrums and behaviors and refused to return the next day. Mark told the principal he'd instead keep Gabe home.

He checked in an hour or so ago, and Tori said Gabe was still "struggling." He refused to do any of his programs, and not even the park, iPad or helping her make dinner would calm him down.

Gabe had a lot more of these "episodes" right after Cheyenne left. The change in routine and missing person from his life had sent the kid into a tailspin. And

Gabe really liked Mrs. Samuelson, so for her to suddenly be missing one day without any warning, well, it was understandable why Gabe had reacted the way he did. He probably thought she was never coming back, just like his mom.

Mark figured Tori hadn't had time to make dinner, so he swung into the grocery store on his way home and picked up a rotisserie chicken and some deli salads.

He wasn't sure what kind of situation he was walking into, so he wanted to come armed with at least food. Feed the poor woman who'd been stuck with his upset son all day.

Mark opened the door from the garage into the house. The screaming only grew louder. It was coming from the direction of the kitchen. He hung up his coat and put his briefcase on the table just inside the kitchen before making his way around the corner.

Gabe was lying on the floor, spinning around on his back, using his feet to propel him. His hands were on his head, and he was pulling violently at his hair. Tears teemed down his cheeks in big thick rivulets, and snot poured from his nose.

Where the hell was Tori?

"I'm here for a hug when you're ready, Gabe. But if you try to hit me again, I'm going to let you go. We don't hit."

Mark walked around the island at the sound of her voice to find her sitting on the floor, tears in her own eyes and what looked to be a big scratch on the side of her face.

Fuck!

She lifted her gaze to his, her eyes filling with more tears. "I'm sorry," she said, having to practically shout over the screaming. "I hate that I can't help him. He won't let me." She hung her head, wiping her tears with her knuckles. "I've done everything I can think of."

Mark crouched down and lifted her chin with his index finger. Her sky-blue eyes were so sad. Did she think she'd failed him? Failed Gabe? Her bottom lip wobbled. She sniffed. He wanted to take her in his arms and tell her it was all okay. That Gabe did this from time to time, and nobody was a failure when they couldn't comfort him. But he couldn't. He couldn't wrap his arms around her like he wanted to. Couldn't run his hands down her shiny, chestnut hair and murmur the things he felt into her ear.

Instead he reached out with his other hand and gently ran his thumb over the scratch. "Is that from Gabe?" It was deep red and at the top was beginning to bleed.

She winced when he touched it, her eyes shutting. She also leaned slightly into his palm.

Uh-oh.

He pulled his hand away, and her eyes flew open. Her cheeks and neck grew a beautiful pink. She knew what she'd done.

Gabe's scream turned into a shrill screech, and they both grimaced, the moment between them shattered.

Her hand came up to where his thumb had just been, wiping away the blood. "He didn't mean it. I don't hold it against him. If anything, that's what made him more upset—the fact that he knew he hurt me."

Mark pursed his lips together, reaching out once again because he couldn't stop himself. He wanted to touch her so badly. He drew his thumb across her cheek and wiped away a stray tear, then he offered her his hand and helped her to her feet. "Have you eaten?"

She shook her head again. "No. And I'm sorry, but I haven't had time to make supper. If you can stay with Gabe, I can quickly whip you up something."

"It's okay. I brought dinner home. There is chicken and salads in that bag there. Help yourself."

She moved over to the bag and began bringing out the containers while Mark crouched back down next to his son. It didn't even seem like Gabe had noticed his father was there.

"Hey, buddy. I hear you had a tough day." It was hard to hear his own thoughts with the moaning sound coming from his little boy on the floor.

At least he wasn't screeching anymore.

Mark rested his hand on Gabe's forehead. He was hot to the touch. Maybe he was coming down with something.

Wouldn't be the first time.

He brought his face into line with his son's eyes so that Gabe could see his dad. A brief flash of recognition resonated in the green, but he didn't stop moaning.

Mark managed to grab Gabe's flailing arms and brought them into the child's chest, applying deep pressure. Then he scooped Gabe up and drew him into his arms, holding him tight to his own chest, eventually maneuvering his son so that he was straddling his father's lap, one leg on either side of Mark's torso, Gabe's arms pinned between their chests. His little boy's moans slowly began to ebb, and his breathing grew deeper and less erratic.

Gabe's cheek fell to Mark's shoulder, his breath warm and even against his father's neck.

Mark rubbed his son's back, gentle, rhythmic circles in conjunction with a soft "shushing" noise. He'd used this technique with Gabe ever since he was a baby. He'd been a colicky infant, and falling asleep upright against Mark's chest as Mark shushed him and rubbed his back was the only way Gabe fell asleep for months.

It didn't matter that he was a doctor and it was recommended that babies sleep in their own bed on their backs and blah, blah, blah. Gabe was his child, and his child was in distress. So Mark did what any parent did who wished they could take the pain away from their child and transfer it into themselves: He sat in a La-Z-Boy recliner every night with his son on his chest, and that is where they slept. At the time, it felt like forever, that Gabe would be eighteen and still sleeping on Mark's chest to fall asleep. But in reality, it had only been a month or two.

Mark also attributed those nights to why their bond was so strong from the get-go. All those nights spent with just the two of them in the living room, their hearts beating in tandem, right next to each other. From early on, Cheyenne had struggled with nursing and supply issues, so they switched to formula by the time Gabe was four months old. So when he was home, Mark was on bottle duty. He was on diaper duty. He was on Gabe duty. He was Gabe's safe place. He was Gabe's provider. Not that Cheyenne hadn't been a good mother at first; she'd been incredible. But Gabe responded more to Mark, always had. When given the choice between Mark and Cheyenne, Gabe always chose Mark.

He felt Gabe take in a big, deep breath, his body slumping and melting deeper into Mark's as he exhaled.

"That's it, buddy. That's it. Big, deep breaths."

Soft whimpers drifted up from Gabe, along with the odd shudder as his body fought to calm down.

Mark just continued to shush and rub his back. "That's it, big guy. You got this."

He wasn't sure how long he sat there, rocking back and forth with his son, rubbing his back and shushing softly, but when Tori gently touched Mark's shoulder, he realized he'd closed his eyes.

"Gabe's asleep," she whispered.

Mark assumed he would eventually fall asleep. That's usually the way it went. But then his night wouldn't be restful, due to the buildup of cortisol in his brain and the fact that he hadn't eaten. He'd be up before midnight with Gabe, and then probably at least twice more.

Mark nodded and carefully pushed himself up off the floor, cradling his son's body against his own. He lifted an eyebrow at Tori, and she gave him the thumbs up that Gabe was still out cold.

Grunting, because he was an old man and didn't belong with his ass on the floor anymore, he heard his knees pop and felt his back twinge. Gabe was also getting big. He'd feel all this in the morning.

He carried his limp-noodle son down the hallway to his bedroom, pulled off Gabe's shoes and socks, then tucked him into bed.

He switched off the light and knelt down next to Gabe's bed, his face mere inches from his son's. Brushing the sweaty hair off his forehead, he leaned in and kissed Gabe twice. Once because he was Gabe's father and a second time for the mother that he no longer had.

"I love you," he whispered before standing back up and moving to the door. "She may have found you too difficult, too much to handle, but to me, you're perfect just the way you are." Then he closed the door and headed back down the hallway to the kitchen.

Turning the corner into the kitchen, he was struck dumb by the image before him. As if she belonged there, Tori was humming a tune and swaying her hips to the song. Her back was to him as she puttered at the counter, probably plating their meal. She had a beer popped open for him, sitting at the table, and the cutlery was all set and salads laid out.

He'd missed coming home to someone. Someone he could share his day with, share his home with, share his life with. He missed the banter over the dinner table, the quiet chit-chat once Gabe was in bed as they just vegged out in front of the TV for the rest of the night. He missed falling asleep next to someone. He missed love.

He cleared his throat. "What tune is that?" He grabbed the beer off the table and took a long swig, loving the taste of the San Camanez Island honey lager. He'd be having a few more of those before the night was over, for sure.

She spun around, her fingers shiny from taking the rotisserie chicken apart. "Ah, I can't remember. Earworm."

He nodded, unsure what to say next.

That always seemed to be the way with them. They could banter and joke for a while, but then suddenly, as if his brain was suddenly elbowed out of the way by *other* organs interested in joining the conversation, he was at a loss for words.

"Almost done here," she said with a slight grunt. "Did you pick the one with the biggest breasts? They're huge!" She grunted again, then let out a celebratory *whoop*. "Got it."

Mark snickered to himself. The chicken's breasts were the last thing on his mind.

He meandered over to stand next to her. There was no reason to stand there and watch her, but he wanted to. He wanted to be close to her. Hell, he didn't want it, he damn well needed it. When Tori was around, he felt a visceral pull more than he had in a very long time. A pull to be near her. To touch her. Protect her. That's when he noticed the scratch from Gabe running down her cheek. Grabbing a piece of paper towel from the counter, he ran it quickly under the cool water from the faucet.

"Here," he said, encouraging her to face him. "I need to clean that up." No, he didn't, but he wanted to be close to her. Wanted another reason to touch her.

"My fingers are covered in chicken juice," she said, heeding his instructions and facing him, her big blue eyes blinking several times before focusing on his face. "I'm okay, Mark. I'm sure it will hardly be noticeable by tomorrow. I know he didn't mean it."

"*Shhh*. Let the doctor work." Gently, he ran the damp paper towel over the blood, mopping it up and cleaning up the area as best he could. It wasn't deep enough for her to need stitches, but she might have a small scar, and it would most certainly be noticeable tomorrow. Perhaps for the next week or so. He felt sick that his son had done that to her.

She batted her lashes, her lips parting just enough for him to feel small little puffs of air on his wrist.

Did she feel it too? The pull? The draw? The need to be near each other? Or was it all entirely in his head?

He didn't need to keep wiping her cheek, but he did because it allowed him to be in her space. It allowed him to be near her, touching her. She smelled incredible, all woman, floral and feminine and perhaps just a touch fruity. He glanced down between them only to see that her nipples were poking hard into the fabric of her long-sleeved black T-shirt.

*Oh, fuck me.*

His cock jerked in his dress pants.

"I ..." She swallowed again. "I think I'm good, Mark." She made a noise in her throat, breaking his trance. She pulled away and turned back to the counter.

"Right." He cleared his throat and took a step back. "Keep it clean. Maybe put some Polysporin on it tonight, a bandage or some gauze and surgical tape. We wouldn't want it to get infected or scar."

All he got was the side-eye. "I've been scratched before. And by clients no less. I think I can manage to not let it get gangrenous."

He nodded, feeling like a total tool. "Okay, I'm going to go change into my sweatpants. I'll be back out in a moment."

All he got from her was a grunt, or was that a grunt from spent efforts as she pulled apart the chicken? Either way, he retreated to his bedroom to escape the stunning woman in his kitchen and the heady smell of her that had managed to encircle him like a plume of smoke and embed itself in his skin, hair and lungs.

When he returned back to the kitchen, much more comfortable in sweats and a gray T-shirt, he watched her wash her hands at the sink, then carry the plate of chicken breasts, thighs, legs and wings over to the table, plunking it down next to the salads.

He pulled out her chair for her. With a flick of her eyes, she gave him a quizzical appraisal, but then seemed to shrug off her suspicions and instead flashed him a big smile and sank into the chair. He followed suit.

"Great job breaking down the chicken. Where'd you learn to do that?" He stabbed a breast and thigh with his fork and put them on his plate. He needed to keep talking to her, otherwise his eyes would drift back down her top and his mind would start to wander, and it wandered into some very dirty scenarios.

"My Uncle Wes was a butcher and a farmer. I spent the summer on his farm one year, and he showed me how to butcher a chicken and then break it down."

Mark paused his fork mid-air. "You killed chickens?"

She nodded. "Yep. It helps you gain a greater understanding of where your food comes from and the work that goes into producing it. You also learn respect for the animal and the fact that they're giving up their lives so we can eat."

"I would have thought you'd go vegan after that."

"Naw. I'm just a lot more mindful of where I buy my food from and how the animals were treated. We're at the top of the food chain. Animals eat other animals. I'm not against it; I'm just against the cruelty. I buy organic when I can. Free-range, ethically treated, that kind of thing. I want to know my food had a good life and then one final crappy day."

He wrinkled his nose. "I didn't check to see if this one had a happy life before his end. I'm sorry."

Her smile was wide and infectious, lighting up her eyes in a way that made the entire room brighter. "It's okay. I'm sure this guy had a happy childhood. At least that's what I'm going to *choose* to believe."

Silence fell between them as they ate. Once again, they'd had friendly banter, jokes and even a bit of a story about her childhood, but then it all of a sudden came to a screeching halt. Why?

*Because you want her, and after a while your brain heads directly into the gutter.*

Mark scooped more salad onto his plate. "I want to apologize for Gabe scratching you. He really isn't normally that aggressive."

Her smile was demure, and long lashes fluttered against her cheek. "I know that. He's a fantastic kid. I know he didn't *mean* to hurt me. Transitions are hard. And he's very attached to Mrs. Samuelson, so to walk in and see the substitute teacher, I knew we were in for a bit more of a challenging day."

"That's putting it mildly."

"I'm not giving up on him, if that's what you're implying. If you're trying to give me an opportunity to bail, I'm not going to." She shook her head and lifted her gaze, leveling it on him. "I'm trained to deal with children like this. I like this job. I love Gabe, and he's certainly not the most difficult client I've had. He just had a rough day. So unless you're dismissing me ..." She trailed off and nibbled on her bottom lip, averting her gaze. "Sorry ... I didn't mean to get so emotional, it's just …" She glanced back up at him. "He's a great kid, and I don't want you to think that one bad day is going to scare me away. I like this job. I *want* this job."

Heat rolled through him and settled in his belly. This woman was one of a kind. An outburst like the one he'd walked in on that night would have sent Cheyenne off the rails. It had been one very similar to that, but in a grocery store, that had indeed sent her packing. But Tori just took it in stride. Sure, it was her job, but she went above and beyond because this was her calling.

Kind of like Mark and medicine.

He always went above and beyond for his patients, sat with them, got to know them, called them at home, gave them a cell phone number he had specifically for patients so they could call him if they needed to. Sure, he was a radiologist and not a surgeon or general practitioner, but he was also somebody who dealt with cancer patients and had to be the bearer of bad news. If that meant sitting and talking with a patient for an extra ten minutes just to make them feel better, he would. Because medicine, healing, saving lives was his calling.

Since a very young age, he would bring in sick and injured animals or help fix a scrape or cut on his friends. For him, medicine had been a no-brainer. He hadn't done it for the money or the prestige of being called "Doctor." He'd done it because he had to, because healing was in his veins, was at his very core.

And working with special-needs children seemed to be in Tori's veins, in her core. It was certainly in her heart.

He went to open his mouth when there was a knock at the door.

Who the hell was coming by at this hour?

He glanced at his watch.

Jesus Christ. It was only seven o'clock. How old was he to be calling it "this hour"? He really was an old man. Thirty-eight going on eighty.

Grumbling about kids on his lawn and the youth today, he got up from his seat and stalked off toward the front door, ready to tell whatever vacuum salesman was cold-calling him to take a hike up Mount Baker.

He opened the door with a scowl only to find three of his friends standing there holding beer, potato chips and more beer.

Oh fuck!

"You forgot, didn't you?" Will asked, pushing past Mark into the house.

His friends from work.

Will Colson and Emmett Strong were doctors in the ER, and Riley McMillan was a general surgeon. He'd invited them over to watch the football game but had completely forgotten after all the drama with Gabe.

And Tori was here.

Shit.

Emmett and Riley sauntered in as well, both of them chuckling.

"Uh … guys …" Mark said.

"I knew he'd forget," Riley joked.

All three of his friends made their way to the kitchen.

Mark cringed.

Not that he was ashamed of Tori. Far from it. But he also wasn't ready to introduce her to his buddies. Sure, Riley and Will were married and Emmett was divorced with zero interest in dating, but Mark also wasn't ready to explain why this sexy woman who was also his employee was eating dinner with him after his son had gone to bed.

"Oh, hello!"

"Whoa!"

"Um … hi."

Mark exhaled and braced himself before entering the kitchen behind his friends. All three of them were standing on the other side of the table staring, yes, *staring* at Tori.

"Guys, this is Tori, Gabe's intervention therapist and educational assistant. Tori, these are my friends and colleagues, Will, Riley and Emmett." He pointed at each of the men.

The woman was mid-chew, but because she was a class act all the way, she smiled, held up her hand in apology, then quickly chewed her food and swallowed.

Even with his friends in the room, Mark's cock jerked in his jeans as he watched her long, sexy neck bob in a hard, erotic swallow.

"Hello," Tori said, standing up to shake each of Mark's friends' hands. "Nice to meet you all." She sat back down. "Are you all doctors too?"

Will and Riley shot Mark a salacious grin as they nodded. Emmett seemed a tad more apprehensive. Though he still smiled at her, he wasn't as carefree and eager as the other two.

Mark fixed his gaze on Tori. "I'm really sorry. I forgot that I invited the guys over to watch the game. This whole thing with Gabe has totally thrown me today, as I'm sure it's thrown you too. You bore the brunt of it all."

She shook her head and stood up, bringing her plate with her. "Not at all. I appreciate you letting me stay and eat. I missed lunch, so thank you. I'll just tidy up and then get out of your hair."

Mark hightailed it around the table, ignoring the gawking looks of his friends. He grabbed the plate from her hand before she was able to open up the dishwasher. "Don't clean up. Just head home. You've had a crazy challenging day and deserve to relax." A thought popped into his head, and he held up his finger. "Hold on." He hustled over to the cabinet along the wall and slid open the door, revealing a floor-to-ceiling wine rack. He grabbed a bottle of very nice Argentinian malbec, one of his favorites, and brought it over. "Here. You deserve it."

"No, no, I can't," Tori protested, pushing the bottle back into his hands. "I was just doing my job."

"I insist. Go, let your hair down and have a glass—or two. You've earned it." He pushed the bottle into her arms. "I've decided to keep Gabe home from school tomorrow, so definitely bring your A game."

Her stunning eyes glittered in amusement. "We're playing hooky? Should be an easy day then."

Mark chuckled. "Fingers crossed."

Her gaze shifted to Mark's buddies. "Nice to meet you guys. Enjoy your game." Then she took the bottle, grabbed her purse off the bench against the wall and headed toward the door.

Should Mark see her out? He usually walked her to the door. But then that just left his friends alone in his kitchen with more opportunity to gossip and speculate.

Ah, fuck it. His mother had raised a gentleman.

Jogging, and all to the snickering of his stupid friends, he caught up with her at the door. She'd just shrugged into her coat and pulled her chestnut hair free to splay behind her. He wanted to run his fingers through the soft tresses, feel it brush against his skin, over his stomach, his thighs as she ...

"Thanks again for the wine." Her smile would fuel his dreams for another night. "Malbec is my favorite."

"Mine too." He held the door open for her, cursing his friends and wishing they'd bailed and that he and Tori were still sitting at the table eating dinner together. That was how he wanted to spend his night ... how he wanted to spend every night.

Her phone started to ring in her pocket. She pulled it out, made a face of irritation, then canceled the call, shoving the phone back into her coat. She flashed him a big smile. "Telemarketer."

"Hate those."

Her smile was sweet. "See you tomorrow." Then she stepped into the cold, the wind whipping her hair into a wild frenzy behind her.

"Good night, Tori."

# Chapter 6

♥

"Dude, you've got it bad," Riley joked, shoving a handful of potato chips into his mouth, settling back into Mark's leather couch in the media room.

"She's crazy cute," Will added. "How old is she? Seems young."

Emmett made a noise in his throat before taking a sip of his beer.

Mark shot his best friend a look. "What? We're not dating. She works for me. She works with Gabe. It's completely different than Tiff and Huntley or whatever the fuck his name is. Lay off."

"How old is she?" Emmett asked. "You think she eventually wants to get married again, have kids of her own? You prepared for that?"

Mark growled. "I have no idea how old she is. And we're not dating. I'm assuming she wants to get married again and have children. How the fuck does that affect me?"

Emmett lifted his eyebrows. "You're getting *awfully* defensive for being *just* her employer."

Mark glared at his friend. "Watch the game."

"Oh, I am. I'm also watching the game going on with you. And something tells me, in the end of it all, you're not going to come out as victor."

As long as Gabe or Tori didn't get hurt, he had no problem losing.

"But seriously, how old is she?" Will asked.

Mark stood up and walked into the adjoining room that was his office. "Old

61

enough to be married and then divorced. Old enough to put her lying, cheating husband through dental school," he called back to his friends as he located Tori's resume on a stack of papers on his desk. He walked back into the media room.

"Yeah, but you can get married at eighteen, and if her husband was older ..." Will continued.

Mark tossed the resume at his friend. Will's big, dark palm reached out and caught it before it fluttered to the ground. He was all grins.

"Says here she's twenty-seven," Will said. "And ..." He glanced at his watch. "Her birthday is tomorrow."

Mark's head snapped up from where he'd been focused on his beer bottle. "What?"

Will passed the resume back. "See for yourself. She'll be twenty-eight tomorrow."

Mark stared at Tori's birthdate. Sure enough, it was tomorrow. He needed to do something for her.

"Twenty-eight isn't *that* young," Will added. "Ten years is totally doable if you're on the same page."

"They're not on *any* page, according to Mark," Riley said. He glanced at Mark. "You gonna do something for her?"

Mark's eyes darted between his friends. "Should I? I should, right? Flowers? Wine? Chocolate?"

"That's romantic shit." Riley clucked his tongue. "Better off to get her something platonic, like ..." He stroked his chin and squinted, not bothering to take his eyes off the television. "Hmm ... what *do* you get a female employee you *want* to bang but can't bang because she's your employee?"

"I don't *want* to bang her," Mark growled.

All three of his friends fixed their gaze on him and said "Bullshit" at exactly the same time.

"What do I get her?" he asked, ignoring them.

"Starbucks gift card?" Emmett suggested. "It's always what I get JoJo's teachers for Christmas and shit. They love it."

Mark's eyes went wide, and his mind began to race. Tori had mentioned a few weeks ago about how she loved a certain organic cream of Earl Grey tea at a local loose-leaf tea shop. She'd shown up with a to-go coffee mug and a loose-leaf tea strainer. She savored her cup over breakfast, explaining it was the last of her stash and the tea was too rich for her blood to indulge in right now.

"You're thinking mighty hard over there," Emmett said with suspicion in his tone.

Mark shook his head. "No, I just figured out the perfect gift."

"If it's edible underwear, you're sending the wrong message," Will joked.

Mark rolled his eyes. "It's not, but now I know what I'm getting you for *your* birthday."

What to do? What to do? Mark had let Tori know last night that he intended to keep Gabe home from school after his outbursts with the substitute, so Tori spent the morning wracking her brain on what they could do all day. It also happened to be her birthday, so she wanted to make the day extra special.

As was the Jones family tradition for birthdays—at least now that she and her sister lived on their own—she did a group video chat with her parents and sister in the morning, and they all "had breakfast" together. She opened her gifts and cards from them on camera and even blew out a candle in her morning pancakes (a tradition her mother had been doing with them since they were small).

Her sister had bought her a new purse from that kitschy boho store down at Pike Place, the one Tori had been ogling a few weeks ago, and her parents sent her money and a new DSLR camera. She cried when she opened it.

She and Ken had received a fancy camera as a wedding present, and it had ignited a passion for photography inside her she didn't know she possessed. Life and the world around her was suddenly full of new intensity, new angles and

63

new beauty she'd never noticed before, and she became obsessed with capturing it.

For the next few years, following the blossoming of her photography obsession, all gifts she gave revolved around photography, whether it be framed shots of landscapes she'd captured or the offering of a photo shoot for friends with children or engagements. She gave the gift of herself, her time, her passion and her unique eye for capturing the beauty in all things.

She'd been positively devastated when she inquired about the camera after Ken kicked her out and he said it had fallen off a shelf and broken. She didn't believe him, but she also didn't want to argue. All the fight had been zapped out of her the moment she came home to find her bags on the front stoop and the door locked.

Isobel told her to go after it in the divorce if she had to. But her parents knew how much photography meant to her and bought her a new one. They said they couldn't stand to see her lose her passion for something that brought her and others so much joy. With tears of joy, she hugged the new camera to her chest like a baby. Because that first camera had been her baby. She never went a day without taking a picture. Mostly of nature, or landscapes, but if the day was nasty and she couldn't make it outside, she'd practice different angles and lighting techniques in her well-lit bathroom with a skylight, taking pictures of the only succulent she'd ever managed to keep alive, in her bathtub with droplets of water on its rubbery leaves.

With a spring in her step and her new camera and camera bag slung over her shoulder, she made her way up the driveway to the front of Mark's house.

It had been an exceptional start to the day, and she was determined to make the good vibes last until she clocked out. Despite her rough time with Gabe the day before, she knew that today could easily be as if Gabe had hit the *Refresh* button and be as smooth as a slack tide.

Mark had said after day one, when she'd knocked, that she could just come right in. She had a key and wouldn't be expected to knock if she worked at a hospital or coffee shop. So she did just that. Hand on the handle, she stepped inside the warm, inviting and homey Seattle home. A house she had quickly come to love and enjoy spending time in.

She wasn't sure if the décor was from Mark's ex-wife or not, but it suited the place. It suited Mark—clean and modern with lots of white, black and chrome, but at the same time, just the right amount of dark wood, warm tones and rich, earthy accents. It was the perfect blending of modern meets comfy-chic that could almost only be pulled off with a professional interior designer.

She heard the soft tunes from the kitchen playing as she hung up her coat. Mark always played music, usually The Stones or Pink Floyd, when he made breakfast. Not too loud, though, as Gabe wasn't a fan of loud noises.

Tori rounded the corner to find father and son sitting at the table enjoying their breakfast: two eggs sunny side up on an English muffin, fruit on the side and a small bowl of oatmeal for Mark, and scrambled eggs, no salt and half a banana for Gabe. Same thing every day. She loved it. She too was a creature of habit. She enjoyed her yogurt with homemade granola and blueberries every morning. She sorely missed her cream of Earl Grey though. The grocery store bagged tea at eight dollars for one hundred bags just wasn't cutting it.

"Good morning," she said, taking a seat next to Gabe and running her hand affectionately over the back of his head. "How did the night go?"

Mark finished his mouthful of egg before speaking. "Woke up crying once around two thirty, but I took him to the bathroom, cuddled him for a bit, and he went back to sleep no problem."

Tori turned to face Gabe. Mark's intense green eyes were making impure thoughts run rampant through her head. "Good job, buddy. And how are we feeling this morning?"

Gabe hadn't bothered to look at her. He just continued to pick at his eggs, pushing more food around his plate than he put in his mouth.

"So far so good," Mark answered. "He woke up in a bit of a bad mood, a little whiny and grumbly. But I think that's because he didn't eat dinner last night and was hungry."

"Then you should eat, bud. I have a whole big day planned for us. Need your energy."

Mark got up from the table and walked behind her to take his plate to the dishwasher. "Yeah? Where you headed?" The smell of him, fresh from the shower, all manly and clean, made her lady parts tingle and her nipples turn pebble-hard. He didn't need to brush that closely behind her, where his elbow grazed the back of her ponytail, but he did.

Had he meant to do that?

She followed Mark with her eyes. "I think we'll hit up the kids' play center downtown first. Entry is by donation and it has a great sensory play area. It shouldn't be too busy, as it's a school day. Then we'll grab lunch at Emerald City Bakery. It has a small children's play area with a cool train table and lots of building blocks.

"The one near Grafton and Wilkes?" he asked, rinsing his plate.

"That's the one. Their cupcakes are amazing. Have you tried the red velvet cheesecake cupcake?"

"I have not."

She licked her lips. "You don't know what you're missing."

His smile was small and coy. It looked good on him. Reminded her of a sexy magazine model who had a secret he couldn't wait to tell. And that secret was that he was wearing the most deliciously tight boxer briefs ever, and all you had to do was unbutton his trousers to find them.

"Where to after lunch?" he asked.

She shook her head, dislodging the dirty thoughts that had invaded her brain. Uncle John. Kiddie pool. Chicken wings. No shirt.

"You okay?" he asked, an even sexier smile of curiosity and concern directed right at her.

She swallowed, shrugged and took a sip of her crappy grocery store Earl Grey before answering. "The aquarium. Then we'll come back here and do some programs and make dinner. Does that sound okay?"

"Sounds like a perfect day. Though don't make dinner. I'm going to pick something up."

Her heart dropped. "You sure?"

That smile again. God, it was going to be the end of her. Or at the very least the end of her career. It made her want to leap up out of her seat, toss her legs around his waist and pepper his face with kisses all day long.

"Yes, I'm sure." His lips twisted in thought. "I'm feeling like something extra special. Any suggestions? What's your favorite go-to takeout meal?"

Tori wracked her brain for the last time she'd grabbed takeout. Seemed like years. It was a luxury she just couldn't afford.

"Hmm ... if I were to have to choose, I'd probably go with Thai. I love all the flavor combinations. They hit every note, you know? Sweet, salty, sour and spicy, and they do it in such a perfect way. What are you craving?"

The look he gave her when she asked that question made her insides liquefy. It was as if they were on the same wavelength and he was craving the exact same thing as her. And it had absolutely nothing to do with Thai food.

"Thai sounds great," he said, not taking his eyes off her. "Any particular dish your favorite?"

"Basil chicken is really good. The more basil the better, in my opinion. Panang curry is another one of my go-tos, but some places don't do it right, so it can be hit or miss."

"Where is your favorite Thai restaurant?"

So many questions. And even though they were simply talking about food and a restaurant, she couldn't deny the intensity that each of his questions was asked with. The room had grown thick with some kind of charge, one she couldn't quite put her finger on, and was, if she was being honest, afraid to.

She glanced down at the table. His gaze was unnerving her. "Oh gosh, I haven't been out for dinner in ages. If they're still around, I guess I'd go to Siam I Am on Crownwood near the Bingo Palace. It's a hole in the wall, in comparison to the other Thai restaurants downtown, but by far they have the best, most authentic Thai food in the city." She lifted her head to look at him again. He was leaning against the counter, studying her.

"Siam I Am, huh?"

She nodded.

"All right, then, thanks for the recommendation. I'll check them out online."

"Oh, they don't have a website. You have to go there and place your order at the counter. Takeout only. And they get busy."

"Can I call and place an order?"

She shook her head. "Nope. Like I said, they're *very* authentic. Like Thai street food, but indoors."

"Ah, okay." He glanced over at Gabe, who was still pushing his eggs around his plate. "Not sure how cooperative the little man is going to be today. You might have a hangry kid on your hands."

The electricity that had been pulsing between them died down. Finally, she could breathe again.

"Wouldn't be the first time. We'll make it work. There is always the smoothie shack again." She turned to face Gabe and made the ASL sign for *all done*. "Are you all done, buddy?" She grabbed his plate and pulled it away. He didn't reach for it. "All done," she repeated, standing up and going to the garbage disposal to dump the rest of his breakfast. No matter how often she tried to feed him leftovers, either from breakfast or lunch or from the day before, the kid had an uncanny ability to know when he was being served "old" food. Gabe would turn his nose up at it or begin to act out and stim uncontrollably until she pulled it away.

Mark was all grins again. "That's the spirit. I'm going to go get ready to go. You guys sticking around for a bit or heading right out?"

Tori gauged Gabe. Even if the kid had a long and decent night's sleep, he still appeared exhausted. His challenging day yesterday was carrying over into fatigue today. "I think we'll stick around for a bit, maybe try to get a couple of programs done this morning, and then head out shortly before lunch. I might try to get some more food into him in an hour or so. The play center isn't open until one, so we have time."

Mark nodded. "Okay, I'll come say goodbye before I leave." Then he strutted his perfect ass, in those sexy dark blue dress pants, out of the kitchen and down the hall, whistling the tune of a Rolling Stones song.

Her heart thumped hard in her chest.

So that's what the perfect man was like?

She shut her eyes.

Uncle John. Kiddie pool. Water wings. Chicken wings. No shirt. Hairy chest. Massive gut. Gross toes.

Okay. Good. Dirty thoughts successfully gone.

She opened her eyes again only to find Mark suddenly back, staring at her with his head cocked slightly to the side. He was holding up two ties.

"You okay?"

Her mouth was desert dry. "Mhmm."

That fucking smile. Goddamn it, why did he have to smile at her like that?

His chuckle swept across her skin, raising goosebumps as it went. "Okay, good. Thought you might have been feeling sick. Either that or sleeping on the job." He jiggled the ties. "Which one?"

His shirt was snow white, his vest the same dark color as his pants. She'd seen him wear this combination before, and always with the black and silver striped tie. Why was he coming out asking for her opinion now? He even had the striped tie in his hand.

"The striped one." She pointed to the tie in his right hand.

He was sending her some very odd signals.

Were they signals at all? Or was she reading into things way too much?

He nodded. "Awesome, thanks. I have a big meeting today and want to look sharp. If it goes well, I might become an adjunct professor at the university med school."

He didn't give her a chance to respond before turning back around and heading to his room down the hall. Once again, whistling that tune. Once again giving her a chance to watch those gorgeous globes of his ass bunch and flex with each long stride.

Ah crap. The dirty thoughts were back, and they were dirtier than ever.

*Hello, Professor Herron. I've been a bad girl. My assignment is going to be late. I've been up* all *night studying for my anatomy exam. Is there anything I can do? Perhaps some* extra credit?

Fuck.

She needed more batteries.

# Chapter 7

♥

Tori's stomach grumbled as she stood over the stove and flipped Gabe's grilled cheese sandwich in the pan. She wasn't sure if she should make Gabe dinner or not. If Mark was bringing home Thai food for himself, the chance was slim Gabe would be interested in any of it. Maybe the rice, but even that was a long shot. So, hoping that she wasn't overstepping, she decided to make Gabe a grilled cheese sandwich, slipping in some pureed butternut squash with the cheese and dipping the bread in an egg wash to add an extra bit of protein. She'd made this for Gabe before and he'd devoured it, even making the ASL sign for *more* once he was finished.

They'd had a good day. Gabe had still seemed really tired most of the day, but he remained in high spirits with her, enjoying the play center, the bakery and the aquarium. Tori had treated them to a mini cupcake each, telling Gabe it was her birthday and that a birthday just wasn't a birthday without cake. He'd smiled like he understood and got icing all over his face.

Humming the same tune Mark had been humming that morning, she turned the stove down and rocked her hips back and forth. Her mind was all over the place as fantasies about Mark flitted in and out, followed by what she should have for dinner. She'd been craving Thai food all day since talking about it with Mark, but she couldn't afford takeout and knew she didn't have the ingredients in her pantry to make anything special. Her sister wanted to take her out for dinner Saturday, which was tomorrow, but they always went to the Sea Shanty for all-you-can-eat prawns when it was her or her sister's birthday. All you can eat prawns for thirty bucks a person—who wouldn't eat until they were sick?

Her parents had given her money for her birthday. Maybe she should stop at Siam I Am and grab a panang. It wouldn't dip that much into her nest egg. And if she made her own rice, she could save three dollars, and it would probably feed her for lunch tomorrow.

Her mouth watered.

It was her birthday. She deserved a bit of a treat. She'd been scrimping and saving like a miser these past few weeks, grateful that Mark fed her dinner because it was one less meal she had to spend money on. She could afford a thirteen-dollar panang. And maybe a spring roll or two. You only turned twenty-eight once.

The door from the garage slammed, and the sound of Gabe's feet running full-bore for his father echoed into the kitchen.

"Hey, buddy. Did you have a good day? Help me carry these?"

She didn't bother to turn around but heard their footsteps approaching the kitchen, the rustle of bags mixed with the sound of the grilled cheese sizzling in the pan.

More rustling sounds and suddenly Gabe was at her side, thrusting an enormous bouquet of flowers toward her.

She turned off the stove and flipped the sandwich out onto a plate before bending down and turning to him. "What's this?"

"Happy birthday!" Mark cheered, coming up behind Gabe with a fancy-looking gift bag in his hand.

Tori's eyes went wide. "What? How did you know?"

His smile was lopsided and drop-dead sexy. "Your resume."

Duh! This man knocked her off her game. He knocked her flat on her ass.

He thrust the gift bag toward her. "For you."

She shook her head. "You really didn't have to. I didn't say anything this morning because it's not a big deal. Not a milestone or anything. Just another day, another year."

Another year closer to death. And she was probably going to die alone.

Wow! That was a dark thought.

"And I grabbed enough food from Siam I Am to feed an army, so go help Gabe wash up while I get everything ready."

Her mouth hung open. Nobody, not even Ken, had ever surprised her like this for her birthday. Sure, her parents celebrated her birth, but that was different. No boyfriends, and definitely not her husband, had really ever given a damn about her turning another year older, even though she always went over the top for theirs.

She clenched her jaw and cleared her throat, the powerful emotions making it tough to swallow. She would not cry. "Thank you," she finally said, though it came out as more of a croak.

His smile was the best birthday present. It didn't matter what was in the bag. That smile was enough to keep her going for an entire three hundred and sixty-five more days. She took the flowers from Gabe. "Thank you, buddy. They're gorgeous. Let's go wash up." Then she took his hand, placed the bouquet on the kitchen table and led him to the half bathroom just off the kitchen, wondering what kind of good karmic act she'd done in a previous life to get a boss like Mark Herron.

"He's about to fall asleep in his cupcake," Mark joked, leaning back in his chair at the kitchen table and resisting the urge to unbutton his pants. "Little dude, you all done?" He made the ASL sign for *all done*.

Gabe mimicked it, albeit sleepily.

Victory! He hadn't signed back to his father in ages. Whatever Tori was doing with him was working.

Mark grinned. "More for me." Using his fork, he stabbed the half-eaten red velvet cheesecake cupcake from his son's plate and tugged the plate across the table. "You were right. These things are good. Like addictively so."

Tori's bright eyes glimmered, and her smile lit up the entire room. "I told you so. We may have already gone to the bakery and had mini cupcakes earlier today. I told him a birthday wasn't a birthday without some kind of cake, and I didn't expect to be getting one today, so I figured why not? Hope you don't mind?"

He shrugged. "Not at all. I'm not *that* strict. It's a special day. Go crazy." He shoveled the rest of the cupcake into his mouth and let the sugar take him into a bit of an awake coma. Damn that was good. An extra mile on his Sunday run good, but worth it.

"Thank you very much again, Mark, for the dinner, flowers and cupcakes. You really didn't have to. I haven't been working for you that long. It's too much."

She knotted her fingers in her lap, struggling to keep eye contact with him, a habit she tended to do when nervous.

Why was she nervous?

Did he make her nervous?

What kind of nervous did he make her?

"You were exactly what we needed at the right time, Tori. This is just my small way of saying thank you. In just the few short weeks you've been with Gabe, he's come leaps and bounds. So thank you." Her modest smile and the color that filled her cheeks made his insides twist and his cock spring to life in his pants. "And here, one more thing … " He pushed the gift bag toward her. She hadn't opened it yet.

Slowly, almost reluctantly, she placed the bag on her lap and pulled the bright blue tissue paper out of the top. She peered inside. A gasp stole past her lips. Her eyes flew up to his. "Mark … you really shouldn't have."

Well, it was either this or edible underwear, so …

She pulled out a year's supply of her cream of Earl Grey tea. He knew she knew how much it was, and the answer was—not cheap. But that didn't matter. It was the look in her eyes and the smile on her face that made every penny worth it.

"How did you know?" She opened up the tin and inhaled deeply, shutting her eyes and letting the rich aroma of black tea and bergamot fill her lungs.

"You mentioned the other day that you had finished your supply, and the way you savored your final cup told me it was something special."

Her eyes grew glassy with unshed tears. "I used to drink Earl Grey with my grandmother. It was the only tea she would drink. And she only drank the expensive loose-leaf stuff. She gave me her favorite teacup, teapot and her entire tea stash when she passed away. That was the last of her tea that day. I was heartbroken, so thank you."

Could this woman get any more amazing?

Their eyes locked for a brief moment, and Mark could have sworn something passed between them.

Had he done too much? Did she think he was inappropriate?

Their moment was broken by Gabe's head slipping off his hand and nearly hitting the table.

Crap. Right, his kid.

He shook his head and pushed away from the table. "I'm going to get him bathed and in bed." He scooped Gabe up and carried him off toward the bathroom.

"I'll clean up."

Then, like a married couple, they went about their business as if they did this every night. He took care of the kid, and she cleaned up dinner.

Domestic bliss.

But it wasn't. He had to keep reminding himself of that.

She was not Gabe's mother. She was not his wife.

She was his employee.

Fuck, it was a slippery slope with her, though. She made his life so easy. Made liking her so easy.

Would everything with her be this easy?

*What do you mean* everything?

Tori nudged the dishwasher closed with her knee and turned back to the sink just as Mark wandered back into the kitchen. "Little man is out."

"Oh, to fall asleep that quickly and soundly."

"I know, right? Takes me ages to fall asleep, what with all the thoughts rattling around in my brain."

Tori put her head down and slipped her hands into the warm soapy water and began scrubbing the frying pan she used to grill Gabe's sandwich. It seemed as though it was taking her longer and longer to fall asleep each night too. Mostly because the thoughts and fantasies that filled her mind were most active as she lay there staring up at the ceiling in nothing but her T-shirt and underwear. Thoughts and fantasies about Mark. About what an amazing man he was.

An amazing father.

A shirtless photo of him and Gabe at the beach was up in their hallway, and Tori found herself staring at it far too often. All chiseled gorgeousness. Perfection in a six-foot-four package. And oh, what a package. At least from what she could tell ... after grabbing Gabe's toy magnifying glass and inspecting Mark's crotch region in his boardshorts a tad more in depth. What a package indeed.

No, she wasn't obsessed *at* all.

He'd fueled her fantasies, her daydreams, her night dreams and all the moments in between. The thought of his lips, his tongue, his hands, his body were what kept her awake at night, kept her hand drifting down her torso as her imagination ran wild. Until her fingers found their way beneath the elastic of her underwear, past the thin strip of hair and into the slick, pulsing heat of her pussy.

When she took the job, she knew it would be difficult to work for such an attractive man, but what she hadn't realized was just *how* hard it would be. And each day she spent with Mark and Gabe, watched him interact with his son, dote on him, devote himself entirely to the little boy, she realized she wasn't just attracted to Mark. She was falling for him.

The past few weeks had been like a dream. They'd all fallen into a happy little routine. She arrived in the morning to pick Gabe up and take him to school. There was happy banter as she sat at the kitchen table with them, had a cup of tea and watched them eat breakfast. Then she took Gabe to school, texting pictures and updates of him all day to Mark. Once home, she and Gabe would have a snack and then either walk to swimming lessons or the park, or one of his therapists would come by for an hour. Mark arrived home around six o'clock, and the three of them had dinner together. Then Mark helped Gabe have a bath, read him a story and put him to bed while Tori did the dishes, tidied up and prepped meals for the next day.

She knew she was going above and beyond her job description, but she didn't mind. She liked being in the house with them. Liked being a part of their world, of their lives. It was certainly better than being alone in a home that wasn't even her own, eating a Caesar salad with chicken in front of the television or one of the two dozen frozen soups or casseroles her mother had sent her home with after Christmas. Mark seemed appreciative for the company, as well as the help. Some nights he appeared dead on his feet when he arrived home, and the smile that erupted on his face the first time Tori told him she'd made dinner was enough to melt her insides and keep her dreaming for days after.

He gave her a friendly nudge, sidling up next to her in front of the sink. He grabbed the tea towel from off her shoulder and began to dry.

She swallowed. Things between them had been changing over the last few weeks. Maybe it was all in her head, or wishful thinking, but the looks she caught Mark giving her and the way he joked and managed to find multiple opportunities to be close to her made her believe it wasn't just one-sided. It wasn't all in her head.

He felt it too.

The attraction.

The chemistry.

The desire.

And what was up with him showering her with gifts, dinner and dessert for her birthday? Did he do that for all of Gabe's intervention therapists?

*You're overthinking again ...*

"So what's on the docket for the weekend?" he asked.

"Not much. My sister and I are grabbing dinner at the Sea Shanty tomorrow night for my birthday."

"All you can eat prawns?"

"You know it! And I have a few modules from the online class I need to get through, then an online class discussion, which is annoying because it's live and as I'm typing a question, so are ten other students, and I'm trying to follow along and then lose my train of thought and end up deleting my question."

His warm chuckle swept across her skin like a summer breeze, comforting and welcome. "I hope you have at least something fun planned as well, besides dinner with your sister. You know what they say, 'All work and no play makes Tori ...'"

"The same as before?"

He elbowed her. "No. All work and no play makes Tori go crazy. Don't study your life away. Make time for fun."

She puffed her cheeks out and exhaled slowly.

Fun.

Fun?

The last fun she had had been the night she met Mark. Her "Goodbye, Ken" party.

"Yeah, and what do you do for *fun*?" She hadn't meant for that last word to come out as provocative as it had.

He huffed a laugh. "Not enough."

Oh, Mama. Tori certainly knew what she'd like to do for *fun* with him. Her brain started to go there.

His abs.

His pecs.

His arms.

*Her* tongue on all of the above.

No. No. No.

Uncle John eating chicken wings with blue cheese dressing, sitting in a kiddie pool with no shirt on and his long gross toenails.

She shut her eyes, took a few deep breaths.

Okay, good, the images of Mark and the way she'd like to have fun with him had vanished from her brain and the backs of her eyelids.

Still scrubbing the same pot she'd been scrubbing for the last ten minutes, she let her gaze slide sideways to gauge his reaction.

He was staring down at the utensils he was drying, a small smile curling up on his lips.

They worked in silence, hearing nothing but the gentle slosh of her hands in the water and the tinkling of utensils as he dried them. But as they continued to work, the tension in the room grew thicker by the second. He didn't need to stand so close to her, and yet he did. So close that their elbows kept touching, followed by her shoulder on his bicep. His *hard,* sculpted bicep. He'd gone and tossed on a black T-shirt and gray sweats after work, and the combination was sending Tori into a tailspin.

"I think that pan is probably clean," he said with a chuckle. "Unless you're trying to scrub off the finish."

Rolling her eyes, she pulled it out of the water, rinsed it and went to put it in the drying rack, only Mark went to grab it, and their hands touched.

Electricity from that simple finger graze beelined straight through her, from her hands, down to her toes and back again, settling somewhere deep in her belly and blooming into a warmth that spread between her legs.

Mark's throat undulated on a hard swallow.

God, even his neck was sexy, with strong tendons and a big Adam's apple that bobbed as he spoke.

"What are your plans this weekend?" she asked, feeling like she needed to keep the conversation flowing. When they grew quiet, her imagination took the reins and drove her train of thought straight into the gutter in Sexyville, USA. And that gutter was filthy!

He lifted one shoulder, passing her the dish towel so she could dry her hands after she removed the drain plug. "Poker night Saturday, then I think I might take Gabe to The Museum of Flight on Sunday. He loves it there."

Right, his "dads' club" and their weekly poker night.

What were they all like? Did they sit around bashing their ex-wives? Bashing women? Or was it more of a support group for the struggles of independent child rearing? Or were they typical men and didn't talk about their feelings at all and just drank beer, ate junk food, grunted and gambled?

Probably the latter.

"Sounds like a good time. Do you really gamble away your money, or is it all for fun?"

He hung up the dish towel, his gaze sliding toward her. "Real money."

She pursed her lips. "Wow. Maybe when I have two pennies to rub together again, someday I can take a trip to Vegas and sit at a poker table. Take in the action. The excitement. Are you any good?"

His smile was coy. "I win more than I lose."

"That's good."

She needed to get going. She needed to get home, get away from the delicious-smelling single dad standing in front of her wearing a black T-shirt far too tight to leave anything to the imagination, and gray sweatpants she wanted to rip off him with her teeth.

"Well, I ... uh ... I guess I should get going. Those fish aren't going to feed themselves." She slid her hand along the cool quartz countertop, letting it ground her and bring down her body temperature. She was in a full-on inferno. The way Mark was looking at her ... it was giving her false hope. It was giving her the wrong idea.

The wrong idea to be bad. To do bad, bad things.

Bad, bad *fun* things.

But, no she couldn't go there.

Nope.

Not ever.

Not with her boss.

Not with the single dad.

His gaze never left hers as his head bobbed in a nearly indiscernible nod. "I guess so."

Was that disappointment on his face? Were his eyes asking her to stay? Were they asking her to strip naked and bend over the counter?

Oh God ... Uncle John eating chicken wings without a shirt on, his enormous, hairy, barrel chest covered in barbecue sauce, sitting in a kiddie pool with water wings and a floaty ring.

Phew. Crisis averted.

Keeping her hand on the counter for balance, because her faculties seemed to have suddenly escaped her, she went to move past him, only her fingers knocked something off the counter onto the tile floor.

"Shit," Tori murmured. She glanced down, only to find Mark's phone, of all possible things, on the floor. "Oh no!"

"It's okay." He bent down to get it.

She bent down too.

Just as her hand wrapped around the phone, his hand wrapped around her wrist. Electricity ripped through her the moment his fingers grazed her skin. A pulse so intense, so hot, so charged she felt like she'd stuck a fork into an electrical socket. She leapt back, dropping the phone and pulling her hand free from his grasp.

"Sorry." He stood up.

Tori swallowed the lump in her throat, pushing down the emotions, the arousal, the pure animalistic lust she felt for the man standing in front of her. "I—I'm sorry. I hope I didn't crack the screen."

He turned the phone over in his big, sexy palm, a roguish grin pulling at the corners of his delicious-looking lips. "Not a scratch."

She licked her lips. "That's good."

His eyes locked on hers. "Yeah."

Tori's mouth parted, little puffs of air coming out as if she'd just run a mile. Her heart beat rapidly in her chest, and her palms grew clammy.

Mark's gaze burned into her. "Tori ..."

"Yes?"

"Ah, fuck!"

And then he was on her.

She welcomed him.

Encouraged him.

Finally.

All her fantasies and dreams were finally coming true as he thrust his hand into her hair and smashed his lips against hers, pushing her back up against the harsh, unforgiving quartz countertop. They were all hands, all lips, all tongues, grappling and grabbing, pulling and unzipping. There was nothing *romantic* about it. It was fucking. It was raw, feral, animal mating.

He palmed her breast over her T-shirt as his teeth grazed her jaw and his tongue drew erotic figure eights down her throat. Her hands fought their way down from his shoulders to the hem of his shirt, pushing it up just enough so she could feel his skin beneath her fingertips. He was hot to the touch, practically singeing her as she drew her nails up from his narrow hips to below his ribcage, feeling his muscles flex and bunch as his hands roamed her body.

She reached the waistband of his sweatpants and tugged it down, feeling his erection beneath her fingertips. He groaned against the hollow of her throat when she fished him out of his boxers, stroking him, reveling in the silky smoothness of his skin.

She was doing everything by feel, but that's all she needed. Her other senses took over as she shut her eyes and let Mark take control. His ragged breathing and hot breath against her skin, the thundering pump of her pulse in her ears, the intoxicating manly smell of him. Every sound, every touch, every smell drove her forward. Drove her deeper into the need to be taken by Mark, to give him everything she'd fantasized about all these lonely weeks.

A drop of precum beaded on the crown of his cock, and using her thumb, she swirled it around the tip. His groans grew louder, more frantic.

Suddenly, she found herself back on her feet on the tile floor, and Mark had pulled out of her grasp. He knelt down and, with an air of desperation to his actions, awkwardly relieved her of her shoes and jeans. Her panties were still on, though they were a sexy nude-colored lacy boy short, so she wasn't sure if he missed them or was in full-on rut and didn't care. He gripped her by the hips and plunked her back on the counter, pulling her forward so the head of his cock knocked the juncture of her thighs.

Damn, that felt good. She shut her eyes again and sank her top teeth into her bottom lip.

His fingers pushed the stretchy fabric of her underwear out of the way, and he explored her cleft.

She was sopping wet.

Tori gasped as spirals of heat pirouetted through her. Her hips lurched off the counter into his palm, encouraging his quest, begging him to go deeper. She relaxed into his touch, her bones and every other part of her turning to jelly.

"So fucking wet," he murmured, leaning forward and tracing the shell of her ear with his tongue.

Tori's mouth parted. Her breathing was already shallow and quick. Little noises escaped her. She was incapable of holding them back. It all just felt too good.

"Mark ..." she breathed.

He lifted his head from her neck. Fire burned in his eyes. Fire just for her. Without a wavering glance, he cupped her butt with one hand, pushed her panties to the side with other. She scrambled to grab his cock and positioned him at her entrance. Sparks of gold flickered in the soulful green as his eyelids slipped to half-mast. He squeezed her butt cheek and drove home.

"Oh God," Tori cried. Once again, after far too long of a dry spell, she was full. And it was by the most incredible man imaginable. She wrapped her legs around his torso, locking her ankles at the small of his back as he leaned her over to get a better angle, hitting her deep inside on the cold, hard countertop.

Mark's grunts and pants filled her ears and spurred her on as his lips fell next to her temple. He was too caught up in the moment, just like her, to do anything but fuck. No kissing, no petting. Just fucking.

"You need a good fucking," her sister had said after everything with Ken had gone down. "Exorcise that motherfucker from your mind, heart, body and bed. Start with the latter two and work your way to the former."

Well, that's exactly that Tori was doing ... or getting. She was getting fucked good.

Mark's hand slipped from holding her panties to the side and pushed beneath the fabric. His fingers found her clit and rubbed.

Her lips opened on a silent gasp. She was hanging on by a thread.

So close.

He grunted. "Fucking amazing."

"I'm ... I'm ..."

Gone!

A million tiny stars burst and flew behind her tightly shut eyelids as the queen of all orgasms crashed through her. She stilled in his arms, squeezing her internal muscles around him, prolonging her release and feeling the luscious girth of him hit her walls, her neurons, her soul.

Her toes curled behind him, and her head lifted to the sky, taking it all in and never wanting to let it go. Never wanting the moment to end. For the first time in forever she felt desirable, she felt sexy, she felt like a young woman not past her prime and destined to live a life alone with six dozen cats and an addiction to The Home Shopping Network.

A loud grunt and exhale next to her ear, followed by Mark halting his thrusts, had her squeezing her muscles around him again, heightening his release and milking him for everything he had.

When they'd both come down off their high, neither of them moved. Instead, they stayed there in their post-coital cocoon for a moment, letting their breathing and heart rates return to rest.

She wasn't sure what she should say, or if she should say anything at all, but the ringing of his phone next to them on the counter solved that problem.

Mark pulled out and tugged his sweatpants back into place before reaching for his phone. Without glancing back at her, he put it to his ear and wandered off toward the home office muttering things about getting another MRI done because he couldn't make heads or tails from the first set.

Tori slid her butt off the cool counter and stepped back into her jeans and tennis shoes.

Should she wait for him?

Did they need to discuss what just happened?

What had just happened?

*You had filthy, hot kitchen counter sex with your boss, Dr. Dirty Dreams, and you did the nasty where you make his kid PB&J.*

At that thought, Tori quickly grabbed the disinfectant spray from the pantry cupboard and a few sheets of paper towel.

She sanitized the counter.

She could be dirty.

But she was also clean.

Mark's voice from the office down the hall carried out to the kitchen. He didn't sound pleased.

She didn't want to ruin their moment, didn't want to kill her orgasm high. So, like a college coed after a hard night of partying, she ducked out of the house into the freezing February night.

She shivered as she sat in her car, waiting for it to warm up.

She'd bet Mark's bed was warm. She knew Mark's body was.

Blowing her bangs off her forehead, she gave her head a shake. It was one time. He was probably going to say on Monday that it was a huge mistake, which it was. Would he dismiss her for it? Should she spend the weekend looking for a new job?

That orgasm high hadn't lasted long. Now she was just filled with dread. Dread and regret.

She slept with her boss.

What had she done?

# Chapter 8

♥

Saturday night rolled around, and Mark found himself at Liam's, sitting around the table with all his friends. He and Gabe spent the day grocery shopping and getting their hair cut, only to have an early dinner with Mark's parents before he ducked out for poker.

As hard as he tried all day, and all last night, he couldn't get Tori out of his head. What had they done? What had *he* done?

He'd been waiting on a call from the hospital and had to take it—in private—when it came in, but he'd hoped she would wait around until he was done and they could talk about what had just happened.

He hardly slept after that. As good as it felt to finally give in to his desire for her, in to the lust, the need, the craving, he knew it was so wrong, and he was probably going to lose the best thing that had happened to his kid—and himself, if he was being honest—in over a year. She could hit him with a lawsuit for sexual harassment, drag his name through the mud and the media. The hospital would drop him; the university wouldn't hire him. And all because he let his dick do the thinking for just a minute.

"Dude, your deal," Liam said, breaking Mark's train of thought and bringing him back to the moment. All the guys around the table were staring at him.

"What's up?" Adam asked, running a hand over his coppery-colored chin scruff, the same shade as his hair.

Mark shook his head. "Nothing."

"That's a starry-eyed look right there," Zak joked. "If I knew any better, I'd say you were in love."

Mark cleared his throat and steeled his face. How did one look when they were in love? He needed to get control over his emotions, over his facial expression.

"What'd you do?" Emmett asked, his tone so fatherly, so parental Mark thought he felt his asshole pucker just a touch.

"Nothing," Mark said, avoiding Emmett's stare.

"You slept with her."

Fuck, his friend knew him too well. He never should have let the guys meet Tori that night. They hadn't let up about her since.

"Who?" Scott asked, his honey-colored eyes going wide with intrigue.

Zak's eyebrows bobbed up and down. "Yeah, who?"

Mark exhaled. "Tori, Gabe's intervention therapist."

"The chick you tricked into a job interview?" Adam asked.

God, that sounded so bad when he said it. He hadn't *tricked* her. He'd bent the truth to get her to meet his son and take the job without her thinking he was coming on to her.

His head hurt.

"Dude, this isn't good," Emmett said. "How did she seem after?"

"I don't know." He hung his head and stared at the faded green felt of the card table. "She left."

"What do you mean, she left?" Emmett's voice had gone up a couple octaves. "Like you kicked her out?"

"No, like the hospital called right after and I pulled up my pants, answered my phone and left the room to take the call. She was gone when I got back to the kitchen."

"You fucked her in the kitchen!" Zak lifted his beer in the air. "Dude, nice."

Mark rolled his eyes. As did Emmett across the table. His friend was trying his best to not freak out at Mark. Why did Emmett have to act like his fucking conscience all the time?

*Because you let your dick do your thinking, that's why.*

"And you haven't talked to her since?" Scott asked.

Mark shook his head. He didn't think a phone call or text was appropriate. They needed to discuss what happened in person. He needed to gauge her facial expressions and tone of voice when he checked whether she was okay and how she felt about it all.

Was she going to even show up on Monday?

"Do you love her?" Emmett asked, his dark eyebrows lifting up on his forehead as he brought his beer bottle to his lips.

Mark made a face that he hoped conveyed his confusion. He didn't know how he felt about her. He knew he liked being around her. He liked how she was with his kid, how she smelled, how smart and funny and sweet she was. He liked coming home to her and his kid, having dinner with her, talking with her, spending time with her. Was that love? He honestly couldn't remember what real love felt like. Things between him and Cheyenne hadn't been good long before they filed for divorce. It was around the time Gabe got his diagnosis at two that their marriage started to go downhill. They faked it for two years, living in separate bedrooms, behaving more as roommates than a couple in love. So he really didn't know what love was anymore. He also didn't know if he was ready to open up his heart again, open up Gabe's heart.

"Love doesn't exist," Liam said, without an inflection in his voice or a twist to his face. He was so deadpan that if Mark didn't know him any better, he'd say his friend was a psychopath.

"Not this again." Adam snorted. They'd all heard Liam's spiel one time or another about how he no longer believed in love, marriage or monogamy, but there was also no stopping him when he got on one of his tangents.

Liam shrugged. "It's a fallacy. Created by Hallmark or Kay Jewelers, just like Valentine's Day and engagement rings. Marriage is an institution devised to mark ownership or property, and monogamy is a social construct that ninety-five percent of other primates, other *mammals* don't participate in. It's wrong. It's unnatural."

Eye rolls and exasperated exhales echoed around the poker table.

"What about love for one's child?" Emmett asked, taking a sip of his beer. "That can't be a fallacy created by Hallmark or Cartier."

Liam held up a finger, his dimples extra deep as his smile grew wider. "The one exception. Yes, love for one's offspring, one's own genes does exist. I mean look at that poor orca mother who carried the corpse of her dead calf for something like three weeks. That's love."

"So love does exist?" Mark asked. He was just happy they were on a different topic. He wasn't prepared to discuss his whopper of a mistake with Tori last night.

All the men exchanged smirks across the poker chips and cards. Liam loved spouting off his theory, to anyone and everyone. Mark had heard it at least half a dozen times.

"It exists, but only in the construct of children. Lust, on the other hand, is a very big part of human, of mammalian nature. The lust for sex, the lust for blood, for continuing on one's genetic makeup, for revenge, for money. Lust fuels us all. The need for fulfillment. But love, no. It's a veil used to blur the true emotion of lust and the desire to both procreate and not be alone. Humans are social creatures. We prefer to be with others. And over the years, the decades, the centuries we've developed some warped ideology that we need to be with just one person for the rest of our lives. And then that morphed into commitment and marriage and women being considered property, and then of course the idea of love. Where one's heart, an organ used for pumping blood and oxygen through our bodies, has such control over our emotions that it controls how we feel about a person."

"It's a metaphor," Emmett said blandly. "It's really all in the amygdala."

"Either way. It's a joke. We're all still animals. Driven to fuck. To continue on our gene line. That's it. Love. Does. Not. Exist."

Adam's eyebrows rose up his forehead, and he puffed out his cheeks before exhaling. The cleft in his chin appeared extra deep. "And on that note, I fold. I'm out of here, boys. Catch ya next week." He stood up, tossed his cards onto the table, grabbed his empty beer bottle to take to the kitchen and left the room.

Mark pushed himself up to standing too. He'd had enough for the night. "You grabbing an Uber?" he asked Adam, joining him in the kitchen and rinsing out his beer bottles.

Adam nodded. "Yeah, just ordered it. Wanna jump in?"

"Yeah, sounds good."

"Had enough of the negativity?"

Mark's eyes bugged. "Little bit."

"Where you headed?"

Mark glanced at his watch. It was only ten thirty. He had the respite worker as late as 2 a.m. if he needed her. He just needed to text Karen and let her know if he was going to be a bit later than usual.

Adam cocked an eyebrow at him as he put plastic wrap over the extra guacamole and placed it in Liam's fridge. "You going to see her?"

"Should I? See if she's all right after last night? It was a huge mistake, wasn't it?"

Adam shrugged. "You'll only know if you ask. Where does she live?"

"Cliff and Palmer, near the Greek Orthodox Church on Westmont."

"It's on the way to mine."

Mark shot his friend a look. "I'm going to grab my coat. Let me know when the Uber is here."

"Liam and his anti-love tirades," Adam said, shaking his head as they drove through the dark streets of downtown Seattle.

"Can you blame him?" Mark asked.

His made a face of acceptance. "No. It's still hella depressing though."

"Agreed."

"Thank God for prenups."

Mark snorted and focused his attention out the window. "You got that right."

They couldn't really hold it against Liam and his hatred for love and the sanctity of marriage and monogamy. His ex, Cidrah, had put him through the ringer.

She started cheating on him with her spin instructor shortly after their son Jordan was born. She kept it a secret for nearly a year, posing as the dutiful housewife, the loving mother. All the while, when Liam was busting his ass at work, putting in sixty-hour work weeks to make partner, she was putting Jordan in gym daycare for hours and screwing the spin instructor in the steam room at the health club.

By the time all things were said and done with their divorce, Liam was a jaded, marriage-hating, woman-suspicious, cynical wreck. Love for anyone other than one's child didn't exist, and monogamy was a big fat joke.

Nobody had met Richelle, and Liam intended to keep it that way. They were nothing but itch scratchers. Fuck buddies. Wednesday night nut busters (Scott's words). So as much as Liam's negativity about love, marriage and relationships grew tiresome on the other guys, they couldn't fault their founder. His heart had been broken, and they weren't sure there was a woman alive that could fix it.

Adam grunted, drawing Mark's attention back to the inside of the car. "I found this the other day. Looks good." He passed a brochure to Mark. "It's a new dance studio opening up. They have all kinds of classes for kids. I mentioned it to Mira, and she's gung-ho, so I registered her for Tuesdays. Looks like they have a class specifically designed for children on the spectrum too."

Mark opened the pamphlet, and Adam leaned over and pointed at one of the registered classes. Sure enough, it claimed to be designed specifically for children on the spectrum, ages four to seven. Gabe was right in the middle of that. Would he like dance? He didn't really dance at home. But when Mark put music on, his son did seem to enjoy it.

"Is it parent or guardian participation?" he asked, wondering if Tori would mind taking Gabe.

Adam lifted a shoulder. "Dunno. They don't open until May, but they look good. You could always email them."

"Hmmm ... Benson School of Dance, huh?" He flipped the pamphlet over to see the picture of a pretty brunette standing en pointe. It said she was the teacher and owner, Violet Benson. He would have to Google her before he signed Gabe up, but it did sound like something his son might enjoy. He folded up the pamphlet and tucked it into his coat pocket. "Thanks for this. I'll give it some thought."

"No problem. So you going to call it quits?" Adam asked, switching gears faster than a Formula One driver. The Uber cruised right beneath the Space Needle, and the whole inside of the car was illuminated.

Mark made a noise in his throat but didn't bother to face his friend. "Dunno."

Outside, the night sky seemed to pulse with a billion stars. The air was cool and crisp. But the scent of snow lingered in the air. If clouds didn't roll in soon, it would freeze hard.

"Do you like her?" Adam probed.

"Yeah."

"Would it be the worst thing for the two of you to ..."

"Dunno."

"Well, you better fucking figure it out soon, because we're here."

The Uber pulled up to a red brick three-story townhouse. A few lights were on, and Tori's car sat in the driveway.

Adam grunted in approval. "Nice digs. You paying her well?" He snorted.

Mark rolled his eyes. "She's house-sitting for a friend."

Adam just gave him a look.

"Shut the fuck up."

Holding his hands up in surrender, Mark's friend simply shook his head, a cocky and knowing smile on his face. "We all know what you're going to do, bro."

Mark opened the door to the car and stepped out, hanging his head down to glare at his friend.

Adam's grin was shit-eating. "Just remember, no glove, no love."

"Fuck you."

He slammed the door to the sound of Adam's cackling.

Fuck. Had they used a condom last night?

Panic licked up his spine. No, they hadn't.

Holy fuck.

He'd never been so careless in his life.

How had he forgotten? How had he not known until now?

*Because you were blinded by orgasms and boobs and the thought of possibly getting more of them.*

Now he had two reasons to be in her driveway. And neither of them were good.

Mark gulped the frigid night air into his lungs. It tasted delicious. The perfect thing to cleanse his mind from the negativity that had been hanging like a fog at Liam's. Not to mention the beer. He needed to be sober. The Uber pulled away, Adam's smirk visible from the backseat as the car headed off into the dark.

Scrubbing his hands over his face, and then up into his hair, Mark paced along the sidewalk.

What on earth was he doing here?

He should call another Uber and head home.

He should text her instead to see if she was okay after last night.

A text was okay, right?

No, a text was so not okay. Not after last night. And especially not now that he realized they hadn't used a condom.

His feet agreed with him, and making sure he didn't slip on his ass on the slick driveway, he headed up the steps to Tori's front door.

Three knocks.

*Rap. Rap. Rap.*

Mark glanced at his watch. It was only just after eleven, and the lights were still on. Was she a night owl?

He knew very little about Tori to know if she was or not. Perhaps because she lived alone, she liked to leave lights on when she went to bed.

He strained his ears to see if he could hear any movement on the other side of the door. He heard nothing.

There was no mottled glass or cut-out windows anywhere for him to check for movement inside.

Should he knock again?

*Rap. Rap. Rap.* This time a touch stronger, a touch louder.

A loud *thunk* from inside had him pausing. Had he woken her up? What did she wear to bed? Did she sleep naked like he did? A million thoughts, ninety percent of them on the dirty side, raced through his mind when suddenly the door swung open.

"Mark!"

He raked her body from head to toe with a slowness that he couldn't control. Committing each curve, each freckle to memory. She was exquisite. Her chestnut hair was piled high in a messy bun on top of her head, a few rogue wisps escaping around her temples and ears. She didn't have an ounce of makeup on, and her cheeks and body appeared rosy pink like she'd just hopped out of the shower. An oversize, threadbare Foo Fighters T-shirt hung nearly to her knees, and her bright red painted toes with rings on them curled into the carpet as a frosty breeze swept past him and into the house.

"Hi," was all he could muster. He heard the door slam in his head as his brain haughtily left for the night. His cock leapt against the zipper in his jeans, painfully struggling to break free.

"Everything okay?" she asked, blinking long, thick lashes at him.

He swallowed hard. "I—" She'd rendered him speechless. He was no longer Dr. Mark Herron, esteemed doctor of radiology. He had been reduced to an animal. His urges were all that controlled him now. His baser instincts. He needed her. He had to have her.

With one hand on the doorjamb propelling him forward, he pushed his way inside, threading the fingers of his other hand around the back of her neck and mashing his lips against hers. He vaguely remembered kicking the door closed.

She didn't fight him. She welcomed him.

Mark pressed Tori up against the wall, cupping her jaw in both hands and exploring her mouth with his tongue, coaxing her to open wider for him, let him in, let him savor her.

She whimpered against him, melting into his touch and acquiescing to his demands. She grappled at him, clinging to his coat. But he could sense her desperation. Her need mirrored his own. He needed skin-to-skin.

"Where's your bedroom?" he asked, his lips tracing a trail along her cheekbone and down her neck.

"Down the hall." Her words came out in shallow pants.

Not lifting his lips from her body, he guided their bodies down the hall, backing her up, pressing a kiss to a new patch of exposed skin with each step.

She pushed his leather jacket off, and he let it fall to the floor. Next was his sweater. Her hands fell to the buckle of his belt just as they turned the corner into her bedroom, but he stilled her efforts.

His cock twitched in protest.

She pulled away from his kisses, looking up at him with curiosity in those incredible blue eyes. Hurt skirted the surface too. Did she think he was having second thoughts?

Never.

Instead, he guided her to her bed, scooped her up and laid her down gently.

"Mark ..." Confusion colored her tone. Her fists bunched at her sides and then in the turned-down sheets, as if she was having to hold herself back from reaching for him.

He shed his boots, his socks, his polo until he stood in front of her in nothing but his jeans. Her eyes drank him in. Roamed his body from head to toe, just like he had her. A rush of color flooded her cheeks, and her pupils dilated.

He smiled. She was even more gorgeous when aroused.

"I want to taste you," he said, climbing onto the bed. "I didn't get to last night."

Her tongue traced the seam of her lips as she watched him prowl toward her.

Starting at her feet, he slid his hands up each leg. She was so fucking soft. Like satin beneath his fingers. Toned legs, beautiful, porcelain skin as creamy as if she'd been dipped in white chocolate.

Hmmm ... chocolate. He'd have to revisit that idea later.

*Later?*

Mark quickly pushed the thoughts of a future out of his head and focused on the now. On the stunning woman before him, devouring him with her incredible eyes. Watching his every move with anticipation and need. Her top teeth sank into her bottom lip, and she briefly closed her eyes as his hands worked their way up her thighs, massaging and caressing. Exploring.

"Mark ..." Her words were barely a whisper. "Please ..."

He dipped his head and kissed the top of her thigh, then the other one. Slowly, knowing how much it tortured her, he pushed the hem of her T-shirt up toward her belly.

Her panties were a dark pink, and he could see a damp patch forming. She was already so wet.

She'd been responsive and wet for him last night, too. They hadn't had any foreplay, and yet when he took her, she'd been ready for him. Was she always like that?

He continued to press kisses over her thighs, trailing his tongue around, tasting her. She shivered beneath him, squirming as he nudged her legs farther apart and settled himself on his belly, letting his tongue wander closer to the apex of her legs.

He kissed right where he knew her clit would be beneath the thin layer of cotton, and her hips leapt off the bed.

The damp patch of her underwear grew bigger instantly.

Mark glanced up Tori's body. She had her eyes shut, her mouth parted, and her ample chest rose and fell in quick successions. Her hard nipples created noticeable peaks in the light gray shirt. He ached to touch them. Taste them.

Tucking his fingers into the elastic waistband at her hips, he gently drew her underwear down over her legs. She helped him, lifting her butt and arching her back, which also caused her to open for him, giving him the perfect glimpse of her glistening pussy. All wet and ready for him.

She had a thin landing strip of hair that stopped at the juncture of her labia. It ran up her mound, but there was nothing more. Nothing to get in his way. He nuzzled her mound, inhaling her. She smelled like whatever fruity or vanilla body wash she used, and it was delicious.

He knew she'd taste just as good.

He wanted to dive in. Get his face drenched in her sweetness, imprint her scent all over him, so it was something that he'd never forget. But he didn't. Patience. He wanted to savor this moment. Savor her. Last night had been quick. It'd been hot as fuck, but it'd been quick. He hadn't gotten laid in forever and hadn't whacked off in the shower in over a week. He was almost ashamed at how quick it had been. So tonight, he needed to make up for that.

His tongue flicked out and hit her clit. Just the tip. It grazed her hood, and once again, her hips jerked off the bed. She arched her back and pressed up, searching for his mouth, desperate for more.

He chuckled to himself. She was something else.

Another flick. Then a swirl. She moaned and churned her hips.

His fingers spread her wide, and he laved up her cleft with his tongue, focusing on the clit but not ignoring the rest of her. She bucked up into his mouth.

Patience.

Both of them.

She deserved so much more than a quick fuck. So much more than shifted clothing and her ass on his cold quartz countertop as he palmed her breasts over her shirt, pushed his sweats down just far enough, and took her hard and fast.

He slipped a finger inside her, curling it up and grazing the soft ridges of her anterior wall in search of that spongy, almond-shaped button that would push her over the edge. Push her over into ecstasy and fill his mouth with her arousal.

She tasted so fucking good.

He added another finger.

Tori moaned. "Oh God ..." She squeezed her muscles around him, welcoming him inside her body. He pumped and scissored, teased and caressed, until his middle finger grazed her G-spot. Her leg twitched.

He flicked her clit with his tongue and pressed up on her G-spot at the same time. Her hips bounced, and her leg twitched again.

She'd be terrible at poker. She had so many tells. She was so close.

His lips enclosed around her clit and he sucked. He sucked hard. Her mewls of pleasure and the way she tightened around his fingers and pushed her mound against his mouth said she was teetering on the edge. He needed to push her over. Hell, he didn't want to push her, he wanted to fling her off and watch her fly.

When he knew that one more hard suck would do the trick, he pressed up even more with his fingers.

She detonated.

Mark Herron was a God.

Or at least he possessed the tongue of one.

Tori's knuckles ached as she clenched the sheets between her fingers, her body writhing on the bed when Mark's lips enclosed around her clit.

Yes.

More of it.

More of his mouth on her.

More of his fingers inside her.

More of him worshipping her.

More of all of it.

Fear and worry had plagued her all day after what happened last night. She worried about her job, about Gabe and losing him. She'd grown so attached to the little guy in the last few weeks, and in her opinion, he'd made a lot of progress. She would hate to lose him, lose her job, lose seeing Mark every day and getting to talk with him, all over their lapse in judgment last night.

But apparently Mark didn't think it was such a lapse.

He was currently face-first in her pussy, his tongue on her clit and his fingers inside her, relentlessly coaxing another orgasm from her. She would give him one.

She would give him many.

She cupped her breasts over her shirt, feeling her nipples. They were pebble-hard. So sensitive. She wanted to feel his mouth there. Wet and hot and oh so amazing.

Her hands traveled down her body, over her flushed skin and to the top of Mark's head. His hair was silky soft and thick. He continued to torment her with his mouth and fingers, plunging them in and out of her, sweeping up through her folds and around her clit. She was tightly wound, even after the orgasm he'd already coaxed from her. She needed more from him. She needed all of him.

Tugging on the satiny strands of his hair, she encouraged him to move his mouth up her body. Slowly, almost too slowly, he obliged, pushing her shirt up as he dragged his wet, hot tongue across her hips, her mound, her midriff, her ribs.

His short beard was soft against her skin as his mouth worked its magic up her body, sending daggers of need through her bloodstream.

Tori shut her eyes and tilted her head back into the pillow, savoring the heat of his tongue, his lips, his mouth. It wasn't until his lips fastened around a nipple that her eyes flashed open.

Yes.

He sucked the hard peak into his mouth. A rush of pain mixed with pleasure sprinted through her body, landing directly on her clit, which was already missing his touch and aching for more of his undivided attention. His right hand came up and palmed the other breast, pulling at the nipple and twiddling it between his thumb and forefinger. She arched up into his ministrations, loving how every touch, every pinch and pull, suck and bite made her want him more, made her want him inside of her.

"Mark ..." she whispered. "Please."

His long lashes fluttered open, and he gazed up at her with soulful, green eyes. His pupils were dilated and his lids hooded. Passion burned hot in those powerful emerald orbs as he scissored his teeth back and forth across her tender bud.

She ran her hands down his back. He was still in his jeans. He needed to be free of them.

With desperation and desire fueling her, she brought her hands between them and began unfastening his jeans. They'd been so quick last night, so caught up in the moment that she hadn't had a chance to see him. She wanted to take the weight of him in her hand, stroke him, see him.

Mark lifted his hips to help her, and within moments, she had fished him out of his jeans and boxer briefs. He was already so hard. A damp bead of precum pearled on the tip, and blindly, just like last night, she used her thumb to swirl it around the crown. He groaned against her chest, lifting his head and kissing her throat and along her neck. His heated breath beat against her skin, making her shiver.

"Tori," he murmured. "Condom?"

Shit. Right.

They hadn't used one last night. She figured that one out pretty quick when she got home.

Her hand paused mid-stroke, and she opened her eyes to glance down at him. He must have sensed her change in behavior, because he stopped too, lifting his head up from her jaw.

"I meant to talk to you about that," he said. A seriousness passed behind his wide-open eyes. "We didn't use one last night."

She nodded. "I know."

"I am so sorry. I've never been so careless before. I'm clean, I swear. Do you need me to get you a morning-after pill or something? What can I do?"

His worry and sincerity touched her.

She slid her hand over the scruff of his beard, cupping his cheek. "I have an IUD, and I'm clean. I got checked right after Ken kicked me out. He was cheating, after all."

The tension he'd been harboring in his shoulders visibly slipped away, and his smile warmed her insides.

Mark's eyelids fell back to half-mast, and he prowled toward her. "We're good then?"

"We're good." She licked her lips, her mouth needing a reminder of how well he kissed. It'd been minutes but felt like hours.

"Excellent." He pressed her into her mattress, his body now covering hers. She spread her legs, and he settled between them, his cock now poised perfectly at her core.

Levering himself up onto his arms, Mark gazed down at her. Tori's heart beat wildly in her chest as this gorgeous, brilliant, incredible man stared down at her with so much passion in his eyes.

She knew it was no more than lust. An undeniable attraction between two lonely, sexually charged people. But couldn't they give in to the attraction? Didn't she deserve happiness? Didn't she deserve to feel good?

Mark made her feel good. He made her feel so good. He made her feel beautiful, sensual and worthy of affection.

He dipped his head, and his lips brushed across hers. She tasted her own arousal and flicked her tongue out for more. He responded in kind by wedging his tongue inside and taking her in a deep, all-consuming kiss. A kiss like the ones they'd shared last night before the rest of their quickie in the kitchen turned into a beautiful blur of panting and thrusting on his countertop. A kiss like he'd given her just moments ago when she'd opened her door to find him on her doorstep. He smelled faintly of beer, but his eyes were so focused that she knew he wasn't drunk. He'd been at his single dads' poker night, and something had caused him to leave his friends and show up at her door.

*She* had caused him to leave.

His desire for her.

Their attraction.

Their ... chemistry.

He wanted her.

Tori melted beneath him as his mouth moved over hers in a way that was both exciting and familiar. As if he had found his way home after a very long time away. How was that possible? For their bodies, their kiss to be so natural, so perfect together so soon? His tongue continued to explore inside her mouth. Every so often, he'd nip her bottom lip or suck her tongue, driving her wild and causing her hips to buck up into him. She needed him inside her pronto.

His golden skin was like silk beneath her fingers. Intense masculine perfection made up of hewn planes and angles, rippling muscles that flexed and bunched as he hovered above her. He was what dreams—fantasies—were made of.

His lips were hard and soft at the same time. Hot, hungry and demanding as his mouth plundered hers once more. Taking everything she offered him and more. With a sure knowingness, as if they had been doing this forever.

"I've wanted you for so long," he murmured against her lips, biting the bottom one and tugging just enough to make her gasp and dig her fingers into the rock-hard muscle of his back.

"You haven't known me that long."

"I feel like I have."

Words were more like pants between strangled breaths.

"Smart, sexy, beautiful, patient. You're the whole fucking package, Tori. You came into my life ... Gabe's life at just the right time. When we needed you most."

Her hands paused on his back, and she opened her eyes.

"Like a breath of sexy fresh air, you brought my family back to life."

Okay, *was* he drunk?

Here she thought they were scratching an itch that had only been exacerbated and not quelled after last night. Sure, she had feelings for him, but ... what were they doing?

He was her boss.

Her fucking hot as hell, virile, manly, brilliant boss who was currently teasing her clit and cleft with the head of his cock.

"Mark ..." Unease began to bubble inside her.

"Shhh ..." He lifted up and stared directly into her eyes. Blood ran hot through her veins; fire flickered in her core. "Don't overthink it, just feel." Then he lowered his head and plundered her mouth with his. Open, wet heat that she could drown in. She lifted her hips, welcoming him inside her. He took her cue and slid home. Filling her. Finally.

They traded moans as his tongue thrust inside her mouth, mimicking the pace of his cock. She clawed at his back, pulling him deeper, closer.

A hand came back up and cupped her breast. His fingers strummed over her nipple like an instrument.

She was lost to the attention, to the pleasure. Every draw of his cock had her body longing for the fullness again; every plunge saw her clenching her muscles around him, never wanting to let him go. He rotated his hips, letting his pubic bone graze her clit. He bit her lip, tugged her nipple, drove deep, and she let go.

A sweet, beautiful orgasm, born of the pulsing, the rubbing, the friction, bloomed like a lone rose inside of her. Wave after glorious wave crashed from the tips of her toes to the top of her head and back again, awakening nerves and building synapses.

She could tell he was hanging on by a thin thread, one she wanted to help him snap. Squeezing her muscles around him as hard as she could, Tori arched her back, pressing her breast into his palm. Her mouth moved over to his ear, and she ran her tongue around the shell.

"Come for me," she whispered.

Mark grunted. "Fuck." He tensed, stilled, grunted again, and then she felt him pulsing inside her. Losing himself.

The second orgasm came out of nowhere, crashing into her just as Mark began to come down from his. She whimpered as her toes curled and the waves rushed through her once more, ripping a response from her center outward.

His forehead fell to hers.

She opened her eyes to find him staring at her.

The corners of his eyes crinkled, and he smiled. "You're incredible."

She knew it wasn't just heat from the orgasms worming its way up her cheeks. She let her lashes flutter closed again for a moment. Mark Herron was in her home—well, her temporary home—but he was also in her bed. He was *inside* her.

Was this for real?

She needed to pinch herself.

But not yet. The fantasy was just too splendid to abandon so soon.

His lips against hers roused her, causing her to open her eyes again.

"You okay?" he asked, shifting just slightly so she wasn't forced to bear so much of his weight.

"I'm better than okay," she said with a sigh.

He kissed her again. "Good. Me too."

She didn't mean to, but she squirmed beneath him, and he took that as her being uncomfortable and slid to the side of her, pulling out.

She felt empty. The fantasy began to fade. She glanced over at his face, relaxed and content with a small, tired smile.

What were they doing?

"Uh-oh," he said, tucking his hands behind his head. "What's wrong?"

Sitting up, bringing the sheet up over her breasts, she turned to face him. "What are we doing, Mark?"

So much for orgasm endorphins. They'd fizzled the moment he slipped out of her.

"What do you mean?" he asked.

She pointed back and forth between them. "This. Us. What are we doing?"

"Well, right now we're taking a break until I can go again."

Her eyes went wide. *Again!*

"You know what I mean."

Pushing himself up to sitting, he took her hand. "I don't know. All I know is that I can't get you out of my head. I've wanted you since the moment we met, and over the past few weeks, I've fallen pretty hard."

"But you're my boss ..."

His thumbs worked delightful magic on the palm of her hand. Who knew a hand massage could be so erotic?

"I know. But I can't help how I feel." He quirked an eyebrow at her. "Am I safe to say you feel the same?"

She bit her lip, glancing up at him from beneath her lashes. "I do."

His grin was boyish and adorable.

"I just know that I haven't felt this way about anybody in a long time, and things with Gabe are going amazing. I don't want to lose you ..." He cupped her cheek. "As a therapist for Gabe ... or from my bed."

She swallowed. "How do we do this then?"

He shrugged. "Any way we want."

"Are you still my boss?"

Was it going to be weird to work for him only to then turn around and sleep with him, then collect a paycheck at the end of the month? Would that mean he was paying for sex? Was this ethical? Her sleeping with her boss?

"You're thinking awfully hard. What's got you making that face?"

"Is it ethical what we're doing? Am I a prostitute?"

His eyes went wide, and his thumbs stilled on her hand. But then he tossed his head back and laughed. "No. Unless you omitted something on your resume." He eyed her warily but playfully, like she was suddenly going to reveal that if he wanted a blow job it was going to cost him extra.

"No. What I mean is, if you're still my boss, still paying me, does that mean you're paying me for sex?"

His lips thinned out into a small smile of understanding. "Ah. No."

"Is it ethical what we're doing?"

Mark exhaled through his nose. "Perhaps not, but we're both consenting adults, and your job is not contingent on us sleeping together."

She lifted one eyebrow. "It's just a perk for both of us?"

His grin grew wider. "You could call it that. You will be my employee from eight to six Monday through Friday, and I will pay you. After six and on the weekends, you are welcome to ravish me for free."

Tori's lip twitched. "Ravish you for free?"

His grin grew wide and cocky, and his eyebrows bobbed on his forehead. "Yeah. Ravish me. Have your way with me." He reached for her. She went willingly, straddling his body. He was already beginning to grow hard again between them.

"My way?" she asked, her hand landing in the middle of his chest and forcing him back to the bed.

He nodded.

She bit her lip. "My way is you, me, and a lot more orgasms."

He gripped her hips and angled her center over the head of his cock. "I love the way you think." Then he brought her down, hitting her deep, claiming her as his.

# Chapter 9

♥

They were halfway into March, but the weather had taken a dip and snow littered the ground. Turned out the groundhog had been dead wrong and spring was not coming early. Tori was thoroughly enjoying her new practicum position with Janice Sparks, her job with Gabe was going exceptionally well, and things with Mark were, well ... orgasmically wonderful. She finally felt like life was on the upswing and going her way again. Now she just had to get through her divorce with Ken and life would be grand.

"Close your eyes," she said Friday night after Mark had put Gabe to bed and the two of them sat cuddled on the couch watching a movie. She'd jumped up to use the washroom and thought now was as good a time as any to give Mark his gift.

He shut his eyes, that irresistible grin playing on his lips. "Are we getting kinky?" he asked, his eyebrows waggling up and down.

She rolled her eyes. "Not yet."

"Oooh ... should we use the blindfold again tonight? You seemed to like that on Wednesday."

Heat flooded her cheeks, and her nipples pearled. She had liked that. She'd liked it a lot. He'd tickled her body with a feather until she was writhing on the bed and one lick away from an orgasm.

She knelt beside him on the couch and placed the box in his lap. "I did like it. But open this first, and then we can have sexy talk." She bounced up and down on her knees in excitement.

Mark opened his eyes and looked down at the box, then up at her. "What's this for?"

She shrugged, her lips twisting in a half-smile. "Just a thank you. Open it."

He lifted the lid on the cardboard box to reveal a collage photo frame filled with images of Gabe. Over the last several weeks, Tori had brought her camera to work with her every day and snapped pictures of Gabe. She'd taken some pretty awesome ones, and after she put them through her editing program, tweaked the lighting and corrected any imperfections, she had them printed and put them into a frame.

Mark's eyes went wide as he picked the eight-photo frame out of the box and held it in front of him with the care one might normally reserve for priceless crystal or a newborn baby.

"Tori …" His Adam's apple bobbed as he swallowed. His eyes grew glassy. "I don't know what to say."

"It's nothing much. I've been playing with the settings on my new camera, and Gabe is such a wonderful model. He loves to pose and then look back on the photos I've taken. I've let him take some pictures, too. He's pretty good." She reached into the box and pulled out two small photo albums. "This one here is more photos of Gabe I've taken, in case you have other frames or want to give some to your parents. And this album is full of the photos that Gabe has taken. He really does have a good eye, particularly for still life."

He studied the images, his hand trailing lightly over the black wooden frame "You've managed to capture all the absolute best parts of him." His gaze drifted up to hers, and what she saw in his eyes scared the bejesus out of her. Was that love? He leaned forward and kissed her. "Thank you. These are incredible."

"I just wanted to say thank you for everything you've done and given me over the last couple of months. My life is so good now. Before you, before Gabe, before this job I was seriously contemplating moving back to Bellevue and in with my parents. Ken took everything from me."

His eyes focused back on her, and he cupped her cheek. "We'll get him. Liam could probably represent you, and he's good. He'll go for Ken's jugular. Or he can refer you to someone in his practice."

She leaned into his touch and shut her eyes. "I just want to be able to land on my own two feet. I don't care about taking him for everything he's worth. I just want my independence back."

"You'll get it. We'll get it back for you. You're already doing better than when I met you, right? You're saving? Back in school. You're doing great."

"Yeah, but my boyfriend is paying for my schooling and he's also paying me to ..." She averted her eyes.

His knuckle came under her chin. "Look at me."

She couldn't not look at him. When he wanted to, the man oozed alpha dominance from every pore.

"He's also paying you to what?" His lips twisted into a half-smile, and his eyebrows lifted on his forehead. He was toying with her, but there was a seriousness in his eyes as well.

"Come on, Mark. You have to admit this arrangement is a little weird."

"Weird how?"

She exhaled and pulled away from his touch. Even something as simple as his knuckle beneath her chin made every cell in her body pulse and scream for more.

"You. Me." She pointed back and forth between them. "This. I mean, I stick around on Mondays and Wednesdays for a couple of hours, we have sex, and then I go home. On Fridays, like today, I stay over but leave before Gabe gets up. It's really nice sleeping next to you and spending more time together, but I feel kind of dirty hiding things. Then you pop over on Saturday after poker night. We stay together until the wee hours of the morning, until you slip out before I wake up, making sure you're home before Gabe gets up. It's like I'm your secret mistress. Like we're slinking around and unable to be open about whatever we are. That it's all about the sex."

His eyebrows went up and his eyes wide.

She started to backpedal. "Not that the sex isn't amazing, because it totally is …" She blew her bangs off her face and shook her head. "I don't know what I'm saying."

Her phone buzzed. She picked it up off the side table, glanced at it and immediately deleted the text message. Ken could not take a hint.

Mark put the box on the coffee table and took both her hands in his, pulling her up to her feet. He reached for a small remote on the end table and hit a couple of buttons. Suddenly, the television turned off and music, slow and seductive, filled the room. He drew her over to the big picture window that looked out on to the city. Against a backdrop of a million lights, the Space Needle stood bright and high off to the left.

"Dance with me." It wasn't a question. He pulled her into his arms, and they began to sway.

She melted into his body, letting him lead her through the steps.

"You are not my *mistress*," he whispered, his lips falling next to her ear. He pulled away and looked down into her eyes. "You are my girlfriend. It's not a dirty little secret, and we're not slinking around. We're figuring things out. Seeing if this works. We don't need to take out a billboard on the Pacific Highway declaring our relationship status to make it official. It's official; it's just private."

She lifted one eyebrow at him. Could he feel her skepticism?

He sighed, taking her hands. "Listen, Gabe loves you, but as you know, he doesn't do well with change and is easily set off. We all need to be eased into this. He knows you as his therapist, but if he suddenly started seeing you on the weekends and seeing us kiss and cuddle, he might get confused. It was really hard on him when Cheyenne left. I don't want to give him false hope if you realize this is all too much for you."

She pulled away from him and stopped dancing, her brows furrowed. "So it's all on me then?"

Frustration filled his eyes. "No. But I've been down this road before. I'm just protecting my son. Please understand that."

It was hard to stay mad when he was just so fiercely protective and in love with his son. His eyes softened, and he tugged her body toward his again, once again setting their bodies off to a light sway.

He brushed his lips across hers before continuing. "I like keeping you all to myself. Don't you like it when I show up on your doorstep on Saturday nights, a pair of handcuffs in my back pocket and a bottle of wine in my hand?"

She struggled to keep her mouth from turning up into a smile. He had her there. Those nights were fun. She usually slept in on Sundays because she was so tired from all the orgasms.

"We've both been burned, right?"

She nodded. Yeah, they certainly had. He'd told her all about his ex Cheyenne and the way she'd left him and Gabe. They'd both been devastated. And Ken had burned her so bad, she still smelled smoke whenever she drove near their old apartment.

"So we need to ease into this whole thing. Dip our toes in. Keep it light and fun until we're ready to take the next step."

Which was?

It was like he read her mind. "We're also working on your independence, right?" His hand slipped down from her lower back to cup her butt. He pulled her against him to let her know how much he wanted her. His cock was hard, long and prodding her repeatedly in the hip as they continued to sway.

"We are. *I* am."

"And I want to help you get there. I want to help you achieve your goals of becoming a behavioral consultant, of opening up your own therapist clinic, fulfilling your dreams."

Her heart thumped wildly in her chest from his words of encouragement.

Ken had never been so encouraging. Sure, he'd made promises of helping her get through school once he was finished his own schooling, but he also made enough utterances about how he didn't think she needed to work, and who was going to look after their kids? To let her know that he'd much have preferred her barefoot and pregnant in the kitchen than a successful career woman.

"Tori." He stopped their dancing. She looked up into his mesmerizing eyes. "We haven't been *together* very long. Just enjoy what we have." He squeezed her butt and thrust his hard-on into her pelvis. "Am I not satisfying you? Do I need to show you just how much you mean to me? Just how sexy, irresistible and dirty you can be? How insatiable you make me?"

She bit her lip.

He tugged her lip out from beneath her teeth and ran the pad of his thumb over it.

Her pulse quickened. Her panties became slick.

She looked up at him beneath her lashes. "Take me to bed."

His grin made her nipples tighten to painful points. "With pleasure." Then he hauled her off down the hallway, only stopping to shut off the music and lights.

# Chapter 10

Mark lifted up the cold bottle of sauvignon blanc and let just a drop or two flow down the neck and into Tori's bellybutton. She was naked and blindfolded on his big king-size bed, spread-eagle and flushed from all her previous orgasms. Her hair fanned out behind her on the pillow like strands of dark chocolate silk, and her fingers bunched in the bottom sheet.

He'd never seen anything more beautiful in all his life.

She squealed and squirmed when the cool liquid hit her warm flesh, causing most of the wine to slosh out of her navel and down over the sides of her belly.

"Careful." He chuckled. "You're spilling it."

"It's so cold." She pretended to chatter her teeth. "What is it?"

"Wine."

"You're wasting wine? That seems sacrilegious."

"It's white wine. I'm not nearly as big of a snob when it comes to this stuff. Can barely stand it unless it's cold as an iceberg."

She licked her lips. "Agreed. That bottle of malbec you gave me was incredible."

"Nothing like a full-bodied, dry red." He moved down her body and ran his tongue up from her ankle toward the tops of her thighs. He reached the V of her legs, where her landing strip called to him. "Though I'm just as into brunettes." He flicked his tongue out over her labia. Her hips jumped off the bed, causing more wine to spill.

"You're wicked." She dipped her finger into her bellybutton and brought it to her mouth, sucking the sweet elixir off her digit like it was chocolate on his cock.

"You're doing that on purpose," he purred, tracing figure eights with his tongue around the tops and insides of her luscious thighs, nipping just enough to get her adrenaline surging. "You know I need a few minutes to refill."

She sucked on her fingers again, her mouth spreading into a devious little smile right before she pulled them out with an audible *pop* and then licked them clean. "I'm doing no such thing. I just wanted to taste the wine."

He hit her clit with his tongue and her leg spasmed. "Two can play ..." He hit her clit again, and her leg jerked a second time.

"The wine is probably getting warm," she chided.

She wasn't wrong. He hated warm white wine.

Levering back up over her body, he bent his head low and swirled his tongue around her flat abdomen, slurping up the sweet wine from her navel and laving at the rivulets that ran down her sides onto his sheets.

When he was finished, he grabbed the bottle off the nightstand and held it to her lips. "Drink." She did as she was told. Then he poured a small amount in the hollow of her neck and over her breasts, loving the way the skin around her nipples and areolas turned to gooseflesh and tightened as the cool wine flowed over it. He took a sip of the wine himself and held it in his mouth, then he took a tight nipple into his mouth as well and sucked, swishing the liquid over the tender nub and letting the mix of temperatures and sensations heighten her pleasure.

Tori's mouth parted, and her hips churned on the bed.

He loved that she was so easily turned on, so responsive to his touch, his presence, his attentions. His ex had not been nearly as easy to arouse or excite. Tori was a breath of fresh air in more ways than one.

He twisted and tweaked the other nipple with his fingers, plucking the peak like he would the strings of a harp.

She mewled when he tugged up with his teeth, arching into his mouth, pushing her chest up so he could take more of her. He removed his mouth and kissed up her chest, scraping his teeth along her throat to the hollow in her neck, sipping at wine there but keeping it in his mouth.

He captured her lips with his and wedged her lips apart with his tongue, letting the wine flow into her mouth, tasting it on her tongue and enjoying the unique flavor she gave it.

Her hands came up from where she'd been gripping the sheets, and she ran her fingers through his hair, tugging on the ends until a dull ache warmed his scalp. He didn't mind the pain. Especially because he knew it meant she was getting all the pleasure.

Her fingers tightened in his hair, and she tugged until he lifted his mouth from hers. He removed her blindfold, and their eyes locked. Heat wormed its way through him, beneath his skin, in his belly, his heart. His chest constricted from how much he cared about this woman. In such a short time, she'd stolen his heart. But he needed to remain guarded. Things were still too new.

She held him there, her hands in his hair, their faces only inches apart. "I ..." Her throat bobbed on a swallow, and he held his breath. They weren't there yet. Even if he knew in his heart of hearts that he loved this woman, they weren't at a place yet where they could say it. Things were just too new. Too fresh. Too raw.

It would kill him if she said it and he hesitated or didn't say it back. The look in her eyes would gut him.

"I want to be on top."

*Oh thank God.*

He smiled down at her, his heart no longer heavy, and worried that she was going to go *there* before they were ready. She just wanted to get her sweet body on top of his and ride him like the cowgirl he knew she could be. He couldn't wait to watch her tits jiggle as she bounced up and down on his cock.

"Absolutely." He rolled off her, sprawling out on his back, just as naked as she was, and tucking his hands behind his head. "Ravish me, woman. Have your way with me."

Sassily, and with a smile he would never get enough of, she sat up and swung one long leg over his waist, positioning her cleft right over his rising cock. She wasted no time, sheathing him inside her. Their groans of pleasure echoed around his dimly lit bedroom.

"Fuck, you're beautiful," he murmured, watching in awe as she began to move in a way that was as graceful and erotic as a professional striptease. She was so confident in her body, in her sexuality, and her fearlessness only made her hotter. She stretched, and her hands pushed her hair up and off her face. Her back arched slightly, and her breasts tilted up toward the sky, her raspberry nipples hard and tight, teasing him to take them back into his mouth.

She shut her eyes, and her top teeth sank into her bottom lip.

She was a sight to behold.

His sight.

She was his.

Pushing himself up to sitting, but careful not to disturb the woman on top of him, he leaned back against the headboard and buried his face between her breasts. She smelled divine. Like Tori and wine. A heady combination of floral and sweet, musky and sexy.

Everything about this woman, *his* woman drove him wild.

Releasing her hair, she brought one hand down between them and began to rub her clit. He loved it when she took her pleasure into her own hands. She wasn't afraid to make herself feel good, and he enjoyed the show. Sometimes when he wasn't quite *up* for business again, she would touch herself in front of him, bringing herself to climax with her own fingers. Or when they were at her place, she would use that impressive piece of hardware she lovingly referred to as "Dwayne," appropriately named after Dwayne "The Rock" Johnson.

Mark wasn't sure how he felt about that, but he did love watching her use that toy on herself. He even loved using it on her. Pushing it inside her slick slit while his tongue ran laps around her swollen clit. Those were some of her biggest orgasms too.

"Oh baby, I'm close," she moaned, her hand speeding up and her bouncing becoming a bit more erratic.

He latched onto a nipple and sawed back and forth over it with his teeth while bucking up into her, hitting her deep and feeling her walls ripple around him.

Her free hand found its way back into his hair, and she gripped him tight, pulling as she found her release. Her body went rigid for a moment as the climax hit her full force, her channel pulsing around his cock, pulling him deeper and welcoming him home. He sucked hard on her bud but couldn't stop himself and opened his eyes to watch her. She really was the most exquisite thing when she came. Her lips parted just so, her eyes fluttered shut, and the most beautiful shade of red flushed her ivory skin. And when she would finally open those eyes of hers, they would be the brightest of blue, content and almost sleepy.

She bobbed up and down on him a few more times before collapsing forward against his shoulder, her body spent and boneless.

"Give me a sec and I'll keep going," she mumbled against his shoulder. "Kind of lost my head on that one."

He laughed. She was so blunt and honest, especially right after sex. He loved it.

"Take all the time you need, sweetheart. I'm happy where I am right now."

And he was. He was finally happy with his life again. He liked where he was at that very moment and didn't want a thing to change.

"Or you could pull out and come in my mouth," she suggested, pushing off his shoulder and staring down at him with a dreamy, dopamine-infused smile.

He put his hand gently on the top of her head.

Her smile grew wider as she pulled off him and slunk down his body, taking him in her hand.

"Maybe just tonight we can pretend I'm your dirty secret mistress," she purred, licking his cock from root to tip. "Or better yet, how about the professor and the student, and I've come to ask for an *extension* or see if I can do something for extra credit."

She deep-throated him, and Mark's hips shot off the bed. "That right there is definitely extra credit," he breathed, then he shut his eyes, slid back down on the bed and enjoyed the best thing that had ever happened to him.

# Chapter 11

♥

"You're sure about this?" Tori asked, wringing her fingers in front of her as they approached the double doors of the big modern Seattle home set in one of the most elite neighborhoods in the entire city. "I'm not *intruding* on your boys-only club?"

Mark shook his head. "Nope. It's not poker night. It's just a barbecue on a drizzling Sunday afternoon. Relax. You were invited."

"A barbecue in March?"

"We're on the West coast. Every season is barbecue season. Besides, it's more of an excuse for Liam to show off his new grill. We'll be eating indoors."

"Are there going to be other women there?"

He lifted one shoulder before extending his arm up to knock on the heavy wooden door. "Maybe. Not sure if anyone is dating right now. Lots of kids though. Most of us, if we're not full-time parents, have our kids on Sundays."

She swallowed hard, but no matter what she did, she was unable to shove the golf-ball-size lump down her throat. It had lodged itself there permanently the moment Mark mentioned the party at Liam's.

Hadn't she wanted them to do more things as a couple? He was introducing her to his friends, The Single Dads of Seattle. This had to be a big deal.

Even though she wanted this, wanted them to bring their relationship out of hiding, she wasn't so sure anymore. And she definitely wasn't sure if this was the best way to do it. What if they all hated her simply because she was a woman? Was this a woman-hating club?

Mark hadn't said if one of the prerequisites for club admission was being horribly burned by a woman—or ex. Come to think of it, she hadn't bothered to ask if any of the dads were gay, widowers or otherwise.

She would find out soon enough.

The door swung open to reveal a very attractive, tall man with brown hair, dark brown eyes and smile that spoke of nothing but mischief and cunning. It had to be Liam.

"You must be Tori." His smile grew wider as he blatantly raked her body from head to toe. Too bad she was in her big, puffy winter coat. She resembled the Michelin man more than a svelte ski bunny.

She tore off her glove and stuck her hand out. "Hi. Yes, I am. I'm assuming you're Liam?"

He winked. "Sure am."

"You have a lovely home. Thank you for inviting me."

He helped take her coat while Mark helped Gabe remove his coat and boots.

"Had to get a glimpse of the vixen that has rendered ol' Marky Mark into a puddle of goo."

Heat flooded her cheeks. What had Mark told them about her?

She glanced at Mark, and he simply smiled and rolled his eyes. "Thanks for inviting us." He thrust a six-pack into Liam's arms. "I know you said not to bring anything, but whatever. Payment for the massive steak I'm going to eat."

Liam's chocolate eyes twinkled. "Sirloin. The best the butcher had. I've had them in the fridge with the rub on them since Thursday night."

Mark slapped his friend on the back, and they all followed Liam around the corner to a big kitchen filled with men and small children.

Tori did a quick survey. Not another pair of breasts in sight. She gulped. Talk about the gauntlet.

All heads swiveled in her direction, smiles erupting on most of their faces. She recognized Emmett, Mark's doctor friend, but he wasn't smiling.

"Welcome, welcome!" Liam boomed, resting a warm hand on Tori's shoulder. "There's food on the counter, more out on the covered patio. I know it looks cold, but I have heaters, and it's actually quite pleasant. Can I grab you a drink?"

"She likes red wine," Mark said, coming up behind her, but not slipping an arm around her waist like she wished he would. Instead he kept a firm twelve-inch gap between them. "The darker the better."

"Dark red coming up," Liam said with a nod.

One by one the men came up to her, introduced themselves, shook her hand and told her they'd heard nothing but good things about her from Mark, particularly regarding the amount of progress she was making with Gabe.

Were they lying just to make her feel comfortable? Or did Mark really spend his Saturday night poker games talking about her?

Liam brought over her wine. "2013 Merlot from Golden Sunrise Vineyard in Mission, B.C. Let me know what you think. A friend of mine is married to the vintner and brought this down as a gift last year."

Tori took a sip. It immediately hit her toes before it even registered on her tongue. She instantly felt a million times better. Alcohol really was liquid courage. "It's incredible," she said, dipping her nose slightly into the glass to smell it. "Very earthy but with a plummy aftertaste."

Liam's eyes glimmered. "That's exactly right." He turned to Mark. "She knows her wine."

Mark smiled but still didn't touch her. "That she does. Hey, who's the new guy?" He jerked his head in the direction of a tall blond man with gorgeous gray eyes. He sat quietly on the couch reading to an adorable little girl with the same color hair, only hers was long and put in pigtails with bright yellow ribbons.

"Atlas Stark," Liam said solemnly. "He works at my firm. Lost his wife in October."

Mark shut his eyes. "Fuck."

"Daughter is Aria."

Mark's eyes opened. "Aria Stark?"

Twin dimples on Liam's cheeks winked. "Claims they'd never heard of *Game of Thrones* when they named her. Spelling is different too."

A tug on Tori's shirt had her looking down to find Gabe staring up at her, a red block in his hand. He pulled harder and pointed at his tower in the corner section of the big, fancy dining room near what had clearly been designated as the "play area." She took his hand and went willingly.

Soon she was sitting on the floor, surrounded by children, Gabe firmly in her lap as she read story after story, and the smaller children brought her toys or random pieces of train track. She knew all the men were watching her. Were they judging her too? Appraising her and whether she was worthy of Mark? Worthy of Gabe? The question was, when they reported back to Mark, would he take their review of her into consideration? Was her relationship with him, her happiness riding on this night?

A bigger lump, closer to the size of a watermelon than a golf ball, lodged in her gut. Her job, her relationship and her fresh start seemed to all be riding on these men and what they thought of her.

It was the interview of a lifetime.

She just hoped she made it through without spinach in her teeth.

They'd been at the party for about an hour when a big man, with thick thighs and dark red hair, came down to where she was sitting with the kids and offered her a small plate of food.

"Thought you might want something to eat," he said with a smile, handing her the plate. "As well as some adult conversation."

She thanked him, diving into the potato chips like she hadn't eaten in days.

"I'm Zak, by the way." He stuck out his hand.

She took it. "Tori."

"You're great with the kids."

She finished chewing before replying. "Thanks. I work with kids with special needs. I love it."

His blue eyes went wide. "That's awesome. What made you get into that?"

"I worked as a camp counselor for children with special needs one summer. Fell in love with it."

He shook his head with a big, wide grin. "Isn't it great when you find your calling like that? When it just hits you like a flyball?"

She laughed. That was one way to put it. "What do you do? Baseball coach by any chance?"

Zak's grin remained big and genuine. "Not professionally. But I coach Aiden's baseball team. I own and run Club Z Fitness."

Tori's eyes went wide. "I love that gym. That's where I used to go."

"Used to?" His dark, thick, ruddy-colored brow lifted up just a touch.

Tori grimaced. "Fell on hard times, had to end the membership. Sorry."

"Ah, we can't have that. I'll hook you up."

They both started to laugh.

She appreciated someone coming over to talk to her. So far, the dads had all just treated her like a babysitter, and truth be told, it was getting a little annoying. Even Mark had pretty much abandoned her to the kiddie corner and been chatting it up with his bros out by the barbecue.

Zak followed where Tori was looking. "You're the first woman to join our little club," he said quietly.

She slowly let her gaze drop from where she was watching Mark and travel back to Zak's handsome face. "I'm not in your club."

He made a face that said he didn't quite agree. "You know what I mean. You're the first woman to be introduced to any of us as a girlfriend. As a significant other."

At the moment, she wasn't feeling overly significant to Mark. He hadn't said a damn word to her in over an hour.

"He doesn't know how to act," Zak said. "Don't let him get away with it, but also just know, he is crazy about you. Talks about you all the time during poker nights."

Tori pursed her lips together. "Yeah, well, you could have fooled me."

"Hey Mark!" Zak hollering across the room made Tori jump. "Quit ignoring your woman and treating her like a babysitter and get in here and give her some attention. Introduce her to the group and be a good boyfriend."

Mark's eyes outside grew fierce, but Zak didn't cower one little bit. He was grinning big time, as were many of the other dads.

Tori made to slap him on the arm, but instead he grabbed her hand, linked their fingers together and then kissed the back of her hand. "And if you don't treat her well, someone else might swoop in and steal her."

Tori's face was on fire, but it looked like Mark's head was going to explode. She liked Zak.

"That wasn't so bad, was it?" Mark asked as they all climbed into his car. "Not nearly as painful as I'm sure you were expecting it to be."

Tori buckled her belt, her head a little fuzzy from the incredible wine Liam kept filling her glass with. Had the glass ever been truly empty? She managed to shoot Mark a skeptical look though. "Once you stopped ignoring me and apologized, no, not as painful as I thought. It was still awkward though."

Mark finished buckling Gabe into his car seat, then swung his big frame behind the wheel and turned on the ignition. "Awkward how?"

She shook her head and watched Liam's house disappear as they drove away. "I just felt like all your friends were judging me. Waiting for me to say something wrong or mess up in some way so that I could prove their theory that all women are garbage. All of them except Zak, that is. He was great."

Mark made a noise in his throat. "Yeah, Zak's a real peach." He tossed on the brakes harder than normal. They were at a stop sign though, so it's not like he did it mid-traffic. "Did one of them tell you he thinks all women are garbage?" He pivoted in his seat to face her, his eyes wide, his mouth open in shock.

She rolled her own eyes and instead turned away from him to stare straight ahead. "You can go."

He shifted out of first and they drove on.

"Nobody said *all women are garbage*, but isn't that what your poker nights are about? Where you get together and bash your exes? Bash women."

"No. Not at all."

She didn't believe him.

"It's where we go to be something other than an ex-husband, other than a father, other than whatever our job is. There are countless resources out there for single mothers, working mothers, stay-at-home mothers. Facebook groups, drop-in centers, support groups. There's nothing out there for single fathers. Sure, there are more single mothers out there, more women with full or joint custody where the dad is just with the kids on weekends, but full-time single dads do exist. But we're not supported. Liam wanted to change that. Yes, we discuss our exes, to a certain degree, but we never *bash* them. They are the mothers of our children. To bash our exes would mean to bash fifty percent of our own children. At one point in time, we loved those women, wanted to create a family with them, so no matter what shit they've put us through, they're not *garbage,* as you put it. We gripe, we bitch, we moan, but we don't women-bash. Never."

Well now she really did feel like garbage.

"Some men, like Liam, Zak, Scott and Emmett, are a little jaded. They were put through the wringer, particularly when it came to custody. They wanted to be more than just weekend dads, and their ex-wives made their lives hell over it. They're not looking for love ... right now. But that doesn't mean they hate women. That doesn't mean they hate love. Well, maybe Liam ..." he trailed off.

126

"But that definitely doesn't mean they hate you or think you, or any woman, is *garbage*."

He reached for her hand and placed his big palm over the top of hers, threading their fingers together. "They all seemed to really like you, if it's any consolation. You were a huge hit with their kids, which goes a long way. And eventually they all warmed up and I saw you chatting with all of them. Some of them more than others. Fucking Zak," he grumbled.

"Everyone except Emmett." Her chest grew tight.

"His divorce is still raw. His ex-wife's new man is a tool. Emmett's daughter hates the guy, which is making Emmett's life hard. He's projecting a bit. He's also just looking out for me and Gabe. It's not that he doesn't like you; it's that he's protective. He'll come around."

She wasn't so sure. It was almost as if Emmett had gone out of his way to avoid talking to her at the party. He hadn't come up to her at all, and when she made a comment about how she used to gnaw on her parents' steak bones when she was a baby, all the other men laughed—except him.

Emmett was one of Mark's best friends. If he didn't like her, would Mark take that as a sign? Her heart was still too raw to go through another tumultuous breakup.

Should she end things with Mark before he ended it with her? Protect her heart?

*You're overthinking things again—cut it out!*

It was too late for her heart, anyway. She was already in with both feet, head over heels for the man, her chest tightened even more.

She loved him.

She loved him so much.

She loved Gabe. She loved her new life and that it included both of them. Gabe was so much more than a job. He'd captured her heart, and every day she spent with him, she fell deeper under his spell. She couldn't imagine having to give either of them up.

"Gabe's asleep," he said. "You want to come over for a bit? I can order you an Uber to take you home later." He took her hand. "I'm really sorry again for tonight. I was wrong for leaving you with the kids. You weren't there as a babysitter, and I shouldn't have left you on your own like that." His thumb grazed her knuckles. "Do you forgive me? Are you going to leave me for the muscly redheaded man?"

Tori's lips twisted in thought. "I dunno. If I date Zak, I get a free gym membership out of it."

With a growl that made heat bloom in her core, he tugged her forward and captured her mouth with his. Their tongues tangoed and lips sucked. The man was one hell of a kisser.

Tori knew she should just have him take her home. She had a lot of thinking to do. A lot of *overthinking,* as was her M.O. She'd dissect her and Mark's relationship until it was spread out into a thousand pieces, then she'd scrutinize every single part until she convinced herself that breaking up with him was the most logical thing to do.

It's what she always did.

Maybe that's why the end of her marriage had been so hard. It wasn't just that she was blindsided and cheated on. It was that for the first time in her life, Tori had been the one getting dumped. Her entire dating life, she'd been the one doing the dumping. Always ending it with the guy before things got too serious, all because she'd analyzed their relationship to death and ultimately decided they weren't the perfect match.

It'd taken her sister knocking some sense into her and telling her to just let love take its course to make her stay with Ken as long as she did. Even then, she could recall at least half a dozen times she'd resigned herself to breaking up with him, only to have her sister or someone else convince her she was being ridiculous and that he wasn't that bad of a guy—boy, had they been wrong. The night he proposed, out for dinner at *Pom,* their favorite restaurant on the water, she was getting ready to break up with him. Instead, he got down on one knee.

She should have ended it then.

*Coulda, woulda, shoulda.*

Should she listen to her gut now? Or her heart? Because her gut was telling her to have Mark take her home, but her heart was saying otherwise. Her heart wanted to spend as much time with him as she could.

He pulled away, his eyelids hooded, his eyes filled with lust.

Tori licked her lips. "Sure. I'll come stay for a bit."

Her heart was an idiot.

# Chapter 12

♥

"Wine?" Mark asked, wandering into the living room after putting Gabe down for the night.

"It's on the counter in the kitchen. Just decanted it."

"Ooh, did you raid my wine wall?"

Her smile was small. "Perhaps. Nothing too pricey though." She'd curled her legs up under her and had her hands between her thighs. It was as if she was trying to be as small as she could. She'd been quiet the rest of the drive back to Mark's place, her mind somewhere else.

It made Mark wonder if any of the guys had said something to her. Had Emmett? He promised Mark he would leave Tori alone.

Mark knew his friend had reservations about Mark's relationship with Tori, knew how he felt about Gabe being in the mix of it all, but he also knew his friend wasn't a complete jackass and wouldn't say anything to hurt Tori. At least he *hoped* he knew his friend.

He wandered into the kitchen and poured them each a glass of the 2016 cab sav from California. One of his faves.

"You're not too buzzed from Liam's wine?" he asked, handing Tori her glass. "From the looks of things, your glass was never empty."

She took a sip and let the wine sit on her tongue for a moment before answering him. "It wasn't. The man is a very generous and astute host."

"That he is."

He sat down next to her and tucked a strand of hair behind her ear, loving the way her bright red sweater made her blue eyes pop.

She stared down at her lap into her wineglass.

She was back inside her head again, just like she'd been on the drive.

He cupped her cheek and urged her to lift her head and look at him. She did. "What's going on in that beautiful brain of yours?"

Shutting her eyes for just a second, she exhaled, her entire body seeming to shrink and crumple with that one breath. "What are we doing, Mark?"

"Drinking wine and cuddling on the couch?"

She shook her head. "No, us. What are we doing?"

Fuck, he was afraid of this conversation. Couldn't she just let them continue to be as they were? They had a good thing going, didn't they?

"I'm glad I came to the barbecue tonight and got to meet your friends, but that's the first time we've been out as a *couple*. That just seems wrong to me. We're not dating, we're ... fucking. Fucking and drinking wine. Fucking and having dinner after you come home from work. I'm a glorified nanny and housekeeper with some sexy perks on the side."

Mark removed his hand from the side of her face and ran it into his hair, tugging on the ends. "Why do we have to be more? Aren't you happy with what we have now?"

"What we have now is a fantasy. It's not real."

"What we have isn't real?" He was starting to get his back up. She wanted more from him than he could give. Why couldn't she just be happy with what he could give her, instead of always wanting more?

"I don't know. I mean ... where do you see us in six months? In a year? In two years? Doing the exact same thing we are now? Me watching your kid, doing therapy with your kid, cooking you dinner and then warming your bed, but only for a few hours, because we don't want Gabe to get the wrong idea." She rolled her eyes before looking away.

"You don't have kids. You don't know what it's like," he blurted out, immediately regretting it when he saw the hurt in her eyes.

"You're right. I don't."

"Do you want kids? Do you want to get married again someday?"

Her bottom lip wobbled, and she took a deep breath. "Maybe. I've never outright dismissed the idea of having children. My career was always my main focus. I just figured kids would follow eventually." She turned to face him again. "Do you?"

He knew this conversation would come up eventually. He'd just hoped they could delay it as long as possible. He shook his head. "I don't want any more children. Gabe is a handful, and we're pretty sure ASD runs in my side of the family, so it's possible another child would be born with a similar diagnosis. Maybe worse, you never know."

She wrinkled her nose. "That's not a bad thing. I would love a child whether they had ASD or not."

And that's why he fucking loved this woman.

"Yes, I know you would. But it's still a lot of work, and ..." He scrubbed his hand over his face. "It already ruined my first marriage. Cheyenne couldn't handle Gabe, couldn't handle his diagnosis, his outbursts, his behavior."

Her sapphire eyes went wide, then she narrowed her brows in a frown that still made her as sexy as hell. "You *blame* him for the end of your marriage?"

Mark took a sip of his wine. This was not at all how he saw this evening going. He'd hoped they would be naked in his bed by now, not having an intense and heated conversation. "I don't *blame* Gabe. The marriage had an expiration on it. It wouldn't have mattered if he was neurotypical or not. Cheyenne eventually would have found a reason to leave. I know that now. But maybe she'd have stuck around and been a parent to him if he didn't have his diagnosis."

"I wouldn't abandon our child!" She stood up, stumbling a bit, so she put her wineglass on the coffee table. "You're lumping me in with your ex because all women are the same, right?"

"I'm not lumping you in with anybody. I'm just saying that I don't want any more children."

"What about marriage?"

"I don't know."

"Then what the hell are we doing, Mark?" She tossed her hands in the air and went to stand in front of the window. "Fucking around? Because although I'm putting my education and career first right now, regaining my independence and getting my life back on track, one day I think I would like to get married again and possibly have children."

He stood up and went to her, but she pushed him away shaking her head. Anger, as well as the wine in her system glimmered in her eyes.

"I'm tired of sneaking around. I told you that. I'm tired of acting like what we're doing is wrong. I signed that agreement you gave me a few weeks ago, stating that I was entering this willingly and you were not coercing me into a sexual relationship with you in any way. You're covered. I won't be going hashtag *Metoo* and dragging your name through the mud on social media. But I want more."

Fuck. His head dropped and he stared at the floor. He'd been dreading this conversation, dreading the moment he told her he couldn't be the man she wanted him to be. Couldn't give her the future she wanted. The future she deserved.

Because she did deserve more.

She deserved an education, a career, a commitment, marriage and children. She deserved it all.

But he couldn't give her more.

He couldn't give it all to her.

At least not yet.

Maybe not ever.

They wanted different things.

Was this the end?

"Tori ..." He reached for her again. "Why do we have to change what we have? It's been working so well for weeks."

"Because normal relationships progress. And I want a *normal* relationship with you. I want us to go out on dates, to the movies and dinner. I want Gabe to know that I'm not *just* his therapist, that something special has grown between his father and I."

She made it sound so simple.

Life wasn't that simple. Was it?

Mark couldn't remember a time when his life had been simple.

College. Med school. Residency. Fellowship. Marriage. Gabe. Divorce. None of that had been simple. None of that had been easy. He went through every day fighting against the current, just trying to keep his head above the water long enough for his head to hit the pillow at night and for sleep to finally come. Only to wake up and fight the current again.

"I'm going to order an Uber and go home," she said, heading toward the front door. "I think me coming back with you tonight was a mistake. We both have a lot of thinking to do, and I need to do that on my own."

He followed her to the foyer and watched her put her coat on. He wanted to make her stay. Plaster her body up against the wall and never take his lips off hers, make her forget all about the idea of babies, marriage and her own bed. But he couldn't. He knew she was right. They both had a lot of thinking to do.

She pulled out her phone to order the Uber. "It'll be here in three minutes. I'm going to go wait outside."

"It's cold outside."

She pulled her gloves on and brought her hood over her head. "I'll be okay." Then she opened the door and stepped outside, leaving him standing there on the threshold watching her disappear into the night. And possibly out of his life for good.

# Chapter 13

Monday morning, Tori arrived at work on time as usual. Only the moment she opened the door, she knew something was off. There was no music playing in the kitchen, no sound of eggs frying in the pan or Gabe humming as he quietly drew at the table. The house seemed colder, too, and the incredible smell of Mark's body wash, fresh from his morning shower, didn't hit her the way it always did.

Carefully, slowly, quietly, she rounded the corner into the kitchen, only to find a woman sitting at the table with Gabe. She was probably in her mid-fifties with short curly brown hair and kind brown eyes. A steaming cup of coffee sat cradled between both hands as she softly asked Gabe questions while he ate his breakfast.

"H-hello." Tori stopped at the end of the table, her hands falling to the back of the chair where Mark normally sat.

The woman's head lifted, and her smile widened. "You must be Tori. I'm Karen, Gabe's respite worker. Mark had an early meeting this morning, so he asked me to come by until you got here." She stood up, took a sip of her coffee and then wandered over to the sink to dump the rest. "Gabe's just finishing up his breakfast. His lunch is packed, and his bag is sitting on the bench over there."

Did he really have a meeting or was he avoiding her? Was this how it was going to go from now on? She would see Karen before and after school instead of Mark. Was that the end of them?

Tears pricked the corners of her eyes, and her throat ached with the struggle to keep her emotions in check.

"Everything all right, dear?" Karen asked, coming up and putting a hand on Tori's shoulder.

She swallowed and nodded, her eyes falling to Gabe. "Has he brushed his teeth?"

Karen removed her hand. "Oh, no, not yet. Come on, buddy. Let's go brush your teeth, and then you and Tori can head to school." She made the sign for *brush teeth,* and Gabe quietly put his fork down and stood up, his eyes flicking up to Tori briefly before he took Karen's hand and let her lead him away.

Tori went about tidying up Gabe's dishes, all the while scanning the kitchen, the desk, the table and any other flat surface for a note from Mark. Surely, he must have left her something, because he certainly didn't text or call her to let her know he had a meeting this morning and wasn't in fact just avoiding her.

Nope. No note.

Nada.

Zip.

Zilch.

Not even "Let's talk tonight" scrawled on the back of a receipt in his illegible doctor chicken-scratch. Nothing.

She picked up Gabe's backpack from the stairs and headed to the foyer just as Gabe came bounding down the hall, his shoes slapping loudly on the tile floor. Karen was right behind him.

"All right. Teeth are brushed. Face is washed. Hair is combed. We are ready for school."

Tori plastered a fake smile on her face and affectionately ran her hand over the back of Gabe's head. "Sounds good. Ready to go, buddy?"

Gabe sat down on the chair by the door and slipped into his Velcro shoes.

Before Tori, he hadn't even been able to do that. He always required help. Now he could do it all by himself. He could also put his coat on alone.

Once bundled, they walked out with Karen. Tori locked up as Karen headed to her car, chatting away to Gabe, who was capable of opening up Tori's car door and climbing into his car seat on his own.

It felt weird leaving the house having not seen Mark that morning. Normally, when Gabe wasn't looking, they snuck in a goodbye kiss. It'd become as intrinsic as her morning Earl Grey, and not seeing Mark or kissing him goodbye hurt her heart in more ways than she could ever imagine.

It was a cold, rainy Monday, much like the mood inside Tori. Thankfully, Gabe didn't seem to pick up on her broken heart and had a great day at school. No outbursts, fits or aggression toward other children. Even Mrs. Samuelson commented on how well behaved he was. Maybe Tori was just that good at faking happiness? Nobody seemed to notice her shattered heart or the fact that she was but a shell of her former self. She'd be faking it for a long time coming.

They finished all their programs at home early with plenty of time to spare before Mark got home—unless it was going to be Karen again. Tori didn't know. She whipped up a quick chicken tortilla soup in the slow cooker and put it on before they headed to the park to go and burn off some steam.

Her toes in her boots ached from the cold, and water dripped off her nose.

A *ping* from her pocket had her reaching for her phone. A missed call from Ken, along with a voicemail.

*Delete.*

*Delete.*

Why couldn't the guy take a hint? She did not want to talk to him. He'd ended it. He'd kicked her out. She'd simply gone the legal route and filed for separation after he drained their joint account and left her without two nickels to rub together.

Her phone said it was almost five. Darkness was settling in, despite that the days were finally getting longer. It was wet, cold and dreary and the low, dark clouds made nighttime seem imminent. They needed to get home. They'd been at the park for nearly an hour, and she could see from her spot under a small copse of trees that Gabe's cheeks were a bright, rosy red.

"Okay, buddy, this is your five-minute warning. It's getting cold and dark, and we want to get home before your dad." Tori held up her hand to indicate five minutes, making sure she had Gabe's attention on the swing as he pumped his body to and fro with all his might. "Did you hear me?" She knew he heard her. His smile dipped, and his eyebrow twitched. He'd heard her. He was just pretending *not* to hear her.

The little dickens.

He was smart as a whip and knew how to use his diagnosis to his advantage. It was easy to *pretend* he didn't understand something or didn't hear someone. Even though within the first week, Tori had learned most of his tells. She knew when he understood something, when he heard her, when he was being stubborn, when he was being coy. She knew when he was triggered and a fit or tantrum was on the horizon. Mostly she managed to defuse the situation or redirect him, but when he was inconsolable, she quickly removed him from the room, held him in her lap, spoke softly, applied deep pressure in the form of tight hugs, and his outburst would subside.

The world was a tough place, particularly for children on the spectrum. But Gabe was incredible. He amazed her every day with all the things he knew and how quickly he grasped new concepts. She also knew when he genuinely didn't get it and needed help. Which wasn't often. Thankfully, he knew how to ask for help, which was what melted her heart the most. He'd cup her cheek with one hand and place his other hand in hers, then he'd bring her over to whatever he needed help with and wait for her to figure out the rest.

Sure, he had his troubles socially, and he was nonverbal. But he understood simple instructions and communicated with the odd sign—when it suited him. He was also wily with those too, using them when he felt like it.

Mrs. Samuelson sometimes found it frustrating that Gabe was so sparse with his use of sign language, and Tori understood why, but to her, Gabe was just an intricate jigsaw puzzle she was enjoying figuring out. And each day he revealed a new piece to her and she had to figure out where it went and how it all fit together. She liked the challenge, and she loved him. As far as jobs went, she'd hit the jackpot.

The park was empty. Which was just how Gabe liked it.

After a long day at school, surrounded by noisy children, structure and limitations, he loved nothing more than walking down the street to the park and doing as he pleased.

And on a rainy day like today, the park was definitely empty. But that didn't seem to bother Gabe. Tori made sure to bundle him up in layers, complete with rain pants, gumboots, raincoat, scarf, gloves and toque, and the kid was happy as a clam to slide down the slippery wet slide on his butt or swing on the damp swings. He was free from having to share, having to wait his turn and having to temper his impulses. It also tuckered him out for the night, and after dinner he passed out, barely able to make it through his bath.

But tonight was a particularly cold night. The wind had picked up, tossing the icy rain into Tori's face as she huddled under the trees. She'd collapsed her umbrella when the wind blew it inside out.

"Three minutes!" she called out, knowing that if she didn't give Gabe a few countdown warnings, he'd lose it, and she'd have to drag him out of the park and down the street kicking and screaming.

She couldn't hear him over the wind and rain, but she was pretty sure he'd growled at her. She rolled her eyes. The goof. As much as she knew he wasn't happy to have to leave, he'd do so without fuss, especially with the promise of a hot cocoa when they got home. And somehow, he always managed to negotiate her into an extra mini marshmallow. For a kid who didn't speak, he was sure convincing.

"What the hell are you doing standing out here in the rain?"

Tori nearly leapt clean out of her skin.

That voice.

A second later he was beside her.

"Ken," she said stiffly. "What are you doing here? How did you find me at the park?"

His smile was triumphant, as if he'd just cracked the Da Vinci code or something. "I still have you on the friend finder app on my phone. Wasn't hard. I've been trying to get in touch with you for weeks. You haven't been returning my texts, calls or emails."

"Emails? Texts?" She played dumb. "They're probably going right into my spam folder. Though they really should just go directly into the *trash*."

"What about my calls?"

Again, she played dumb and simply shrugged. "No clue."

He made some kind of a noise in his throat. "Mature."

"Perhaps you should take the hint that I'm not interested in talking to you."

"It's not always about what you want, Tori."

It was never about what she wanted. It was always all about Ken.

Growling, she pulled the hood of her jacket tighter around her face to block out the wind and rain. "What do you want?"

"I want to talk."

"Then do it through lawyers. You made it very clear you were finished with me."

An unsure look crossed his face. "Do you have a lawyer?"

No. Not yet. She couldn't afford one. Did Liam do pro bono work? Did he have a friend discount? She'd have to talk to Mark about finding a lawyer.

"Sure do," she lied. "And he's good."

Ken swallowed. "Can we please just talk?"

Glaring at him, she exhaled. "Fine. You have five minutes."

Gabe's head swiveled around.

"Yes, Gabe." She held up five gloved fingers. "You get five extra minutes while I have a chat with Mr. Snider."

"*Dr.* Snider," he corrected.

"Oh for fuck's sake. Talk, before I change my mind." She refused to look at him. The man didn't deserve her eye contact. After what he'd done to her, what he'd put her through, he didn't deserve a moment of her fucking time.

"I want my engagement ring back."

Okay, now she *had* to look at him. Her mouth opened in disgust, rain landing on her tongue and lips.

"And the earrings my mother gave you as a gift last Christmas."

"Excuse me?"

Was he out of his goddamn mind?

"What?" He had the audacity to appear surprised. Did he honestly think she'd just shrug and hand it all over? She'd been holding on to that ring in case her financial situation grew dire and she needed to make a decision between electricity and food. And the earrings? Those had been a gift from his mother. They had nothing to do with Ken. His mother, one of the kindest women Tori had ever met, had generously given Tori a pair of stunning diamond chandelier earrings last Christmas. They had been hers, a gift from her own late mother, but she didn't wear extravagant jewelry anymore and Ken's sister didn't want them. In MaryAnne's words, "something so beautiful should be worn by someone just as beautiful." So she'd given them to Tori. She'd even taken Tori aside and said that these had nothing to do with Ken and there was zero expectation to get them back, no matter the circumstances.

Had MaryAnne known about Ken's cheating ways already? Was she sending Tori a message?

"Why do you want the earrings?" he asked. "Aren't they just a reminder of my family? Of me?"

"I *love* your family. I love your parents, your sister, your brother. And as far as I know, none of them are happy with what you did to me. Every single one of them has reached out and told me how disappointed they are with you and how they still want to be in my life. They all messaged me on my birthday. Your mother even mailed me a card."

He shifted back and forth on his feet, obviously uncomfortable with the fact that Tori had been in contact with his family. But what he didn't seem to understand was that up until recently, they had also been *her* family. She and Ken were married. She was a member of the Snider family. The only thing she hadn't done was take his name. Not that Jones was a last name that needed to be preserved because it was unique or anything, but she and her sister were the last of their family line. She'd also had a horrible teacher in high school named Mrs. Snider (no relation to Ken's family), so the thought of becoming Mrs. Snider gave her nightmares.

Ken lifted his chin, raindrops dripping off his longish nose and lashes. His dark brown eyes held zero compassion for her. It was hard to believe this man had once claimed to love, honor and cherish her until death do they part. Now he just looked at her like a wad of gum he couldn't get off the bottom of his shoe.

"I'm aware of how my family feels. But I still want the engagement ring back. Wedding ring too."

"Why?" Was he hard up for cash? He was a dentist, for crying out loud. The man couldn't be hurting that bad, especially since she'd covered the majority of his schooling, and then he'd drained their savings to pay off his student loans.

Another look of unease crossed his damp and flushed face. "Nicole has very expensive tastes."

Ah. It was his little hoochie of a mistress.

"And your salary as a dentist can't keep her in the lace and silk she's become accustomed to?"

"Those earrings were a family heirloom. It's not right that you should have them."

"And the ring? I don't remember that being an heirloom. Your mother's ring went to your brother. My ring came from a jewelry store." A gloved hand slid into hers. Glancing down, she found Gabe looking up at both of them with rosy cheeks and confusion. He blinked his long, damp lashes and tugged at her hand. He was ready to go. "Just a second, buddy. I'm almost done."

His jaw clenched.

"I know. I'm cold too. How about *seven* marshmallows instead of five?"

The kid seemed barely placated, but he twisted his lips and glanced out toward the park.

"You can go back and play more if you want."

He released her hand and returned to the swings, though he didn't pump with enthusiasm like before. He simply splayed his belly across a swing seat and twisted back and forth, kicking up mud in the puddle below.

"We can do this the easy way, where you just give them to me, or we can do this the hard way, where I come after you with my lawyers," Ken said, drawing her attention away from Gabe and back to the insufferable man she'd once been head over heels for.

How could she have been so wrong?

Tori did her best to beat down the fury that wanted to erupt like a volcano. She kept her voice low and level as she asked, "Why are you doing this? All I ever did was love you."

His top lip curled. "Please. You were always looking for a way to end it. Nobody is ever good enough for *Victoria Jones*. Unlike the endless stream of schmucks before me, I decided to be the *dumper* rather than the *dumpee*."

"Then why didn't you just end it? Why didn't you just hand me divorce papers instead of taking away everything from me? Cheating on me? Leaving me penniless and homeless."

He shrugged. "It was Nicole's idea."

Typical Ken. Never the one at fault. Always quick to deflect the blame.

She nodded, not believing him for a second. "I'm sure."

"Believe what you want," he said, appearing almost bored. "I told her how you were always so focused on work and having a career rather than a family. Not her. We're already trying for a baby. We have the same goals. Same priorities."

Tori felt like she was going to be sick.

"It was her idea to throw all my things out of the apartment? Change the locks and drain our bank account? That seems more up your alley."

An evil yet wistful glint flashed in his eyes. "She's creative, I'll give her that."

She's evil, Tori would give her that. "I wasn't focused on *my* career. I was focused on *yours*. I put you through school! I worked three jobs, did all the cooking and the cleaning, and you promised that when you finished dental school, it would be *my* turn. I put my life, my education, my career on hold for you. And now you want to take *more* from me?"

"Wouldn't you rather be rid of me completely?" The man was a psychopath.

Hoping that her glare was as hate-filled as she felt, she whispered, "Bring on the lawyers." Then she headed to grab Gabe.

"You'll be sorry. You had your chance to do the right thing. To be civil about this!" he called after her. "My lawyer is going to drag you through the mud. I know you're sleeping with your boss. I know you're sleeping with that kid's dad. I've seen his car at your place."

Tori spun around and hollered back through the rain, "Have you been stalking me?"

His mouth turned up into the ugliest sneer. "Keeping tabs."

"You make me sick."

"What's he paying you for? Babysitting and sex? Are you a whore now, Tori? Been reduced to nothing more than a babysitter and the dad's sidepiece."

Lava everywhere. Ash filled the hole where her heart had once been. Molten hot rage flowed through her as she raced back up to Ken. Her hand came up and landed with a hard, wet smack across his cheek. It stung her palm, but the pain was comforting. She hoped to holy hell it felt ten times worse for him.

"Fucking bitch!"

She went for another smack, but he grabbed her arm this time. "I could charge you with assault," he threatened, his grip on her arm firm and causing a sharp shard of pain to sprint up into her shoulder.

"Let go of me!" She wrenched free and squared off with him. "You're an asshole."

Contempt fell across his face. "And you appear to have lost your kid." With a cackle, he popped up the collar of his coat, turned his back on her and left the park.

Tori spun around expecting to find Gabe still spinning around on the swing, or back up on the slide, but he was nowhere to be found. Night had fallen completely, and although there were a couple of street lamps lighting the park, it wasn't enough.

Oh no!

"Gabe!" she called, racing around the park. The wind carried her voice away. She yelled louder. "Gabe!"

The rain picked up. Drops the size of gumballs hit her in the face. She was soaked through, but none of that mattered. She had to find him.

How could Ken leave her? Was he really that soulless?

*Yes, the man has no heart.*

A screech and horn honk from out on the street made her run out of the fenced park and to the sidewalk.

No!

Gabe was on the grassy median on the boulevard. Panic painted his face as he realized the danger he was in.

It was rush hour.

There were three lanes of traffic on either side.

The rain was coming down hard enough to blur even 20/20 vision, and he was not wearing any reflective clothing. His coat was dark blue, and his rain pants were black.

If she called his name, he could dart out into traffic to get to her.

Nobody was stopping. Because nobody saw him.

He just kept pacing, up and down the grass. She could tell, even across the road in the dark and rain, that he was crying. Anguish scrunched up his innocent features as he struggled to process his situation.

She had to get to him.

She glanced up and down the road. The nearest crosswalk was too far away. It would take him out of her sight, and she couldn't take her eyes off him. She wasn't in enough reflective clothing either. It wasn't safe for her to step out and stall cars so she could cross.

"TOOOOORI!"

She spun around at her name.

He spotted her, and he was calling her name.

"TOOOOOOOORI!"

He was saying her name.

The boy had never uttered a single word in his life, and he was calling her name.

"TOOOOOOOORI!" His eyes darted over the cars, and he took a hesitant step forward.

She held her hands out to stop him, shaking her head wildly. "NO!" She hollered back. "NOT SAFE! Stay!" He understood *not safe*. They'd used that before when crossing the road or walking down along the river or on the dock. He was no dummy when it came to safety.

So why had he run away and out into the road?

Sobs wracked his body, and he began to bounce on his heels, his head shaking violently. "TOOOOOOORI!"

Tires screeched on the other side of the road, and a dark car stopped mid-traffic, immediately tossing on its hazard lights.

Oh thank God. Someone finally saw him.

Relief flooded Tori's body.

The driver's side door opened and out stepped Mark.

Her heart stopped.

"What in the FUCK were you thinking?" Mark's voice boomed around the high-ceiling living room back at the house. His face was red, twisted, and his eyes burned hot. The man didn't look at her with an ounce of love or compassion. His heart was now full of rage, rage toward her and how her actions, her choices had endangered Gabe. He couldn't make her feel any worse than she already did. She wanted to crawl into the nearest gutter and never come out.

Gabe had been given hot cocoa, supper, a bath and been put to bed. All the while Tori had done as she'd been told and sat on the couch in her wet clothes and waited for Mark to see to his son.

She felt like a child herself, waiting for the belt or wooden spoon.

Tears streamed down her face, and she shook her head. "I'm so sorry."

"You're sorry? You're *sorry?* Sorry doesn't fucking cut it. You nearly got my son killed."

She nodded. "I know. It was Ken. He found us at the park and … "

He cut her off. "So you let your personal problems compromise the safety of my child? You brought your personal bullshit to the workplace?" He paced back and forth in front of her, his face a scary shade of red and his hair standing straight up as if he'd run his fingers through it a dozen times and pulled on the ends. "You're fucking fired!"

She lifted her head. "Mark … please."

He held his hand up to stop her. "Don't. Don't even try. You let … our *situation*"—he pointed back and forth between the two of them—"cloud your responsibilities. You got lazy. Figured now that you're fucking your boss you didn't have to watch his son, didn't have to do your fucking job! I pay you so fucking well, pay for your schooling, you should have your eyes glued to that child for the entire duration of your shift. But no, now that we started sleeping together, you figured you could slack off. *Mark won't care that I fucked around on shift, not as long as I get down on my knees later tonight."*

A thousand arrows pierced her heart. How could he say those things to her? How could he think that? She fought back more tears, but it was a lost cause. Words choked out of her as she struggled with the idea of dropping to the floor and begging for a second chance. But she knew she'd never get one. The way he was looking at her, glowering at her, said he never wanted to see her again. She wiped the back of her wrist beneath her nose and whispered, "It wasn't like that. Ken came, he threatened lawyers, demanded I give back my engagement ring. He was so cruel, so heartless. Then things got ... physical." She hung her head down.

"Did you kiss him in front of Gabe?" A new level of fury laced his tone. Was that jealousy as well?

Her head popped back up. "No! Of course not. I slapped him, and he grabbed my arm and twisted it."

A modicum of relief glimmered in his eyes, and then it was gone. "So you were fighting with your ex when you should have been watching my kid?"

"I—I took my eyes off him for a second, I swear. He was right behind me on the swings. Gabe has never bolted from me before. He knows road safety. He's a smart kid."

"But he also has fucking autism and is unpredictable!"

"Please ... don't do this."

He glared down at her. "Effective immediately, I no longer require your *services*." He spun around, showing her his back. "You're dismissed. I will have my accountant pay you for the time you've already worked this month."

Then he stood there, staring out the window into the dark, waiting for her to leave, unwilling to hear anything else she had to say, unwilling to even look at her.

Mark Herron was done with her.

She'd lost everything—Mark, Gabe, her job, her education. Why not say her piece? Stand up for herself. She hadn't done it nearly enough with Ken, and look where that got her. Even if she and Mark were over, she needed to keep building and strengthening her spine, keep striving for her independence. Besides, she couldn't lose more, she'd already lost everything. She couldn't get more fired. Taking a deep breath, she stood up and faced his back. "There were two of us in this relationship, Mark. You and me. The boss and the employee."

He didn't turn around, but she noticed his body stiffen.

"I messed up and I'm owning that, but you're not without guilt here either. You treated me like your dirty little mistress. You used me. As much as you said you weren't going to do that, you did. You wanted to maintain the status quo because it's what worked for *you*. It's what was easy for *you*. To hell with what I wanted. I'm sure that if I'd allowed it, you would have been fine keeping me on as a side-piece until Gabe was eighteen. Nothing more than an employee during the week and your secret mistress on the weekends. No muss no fuss." She shook her head, watching the way his back muscles tensed as the truth of her words hit him. "You can be mad at me for taking my eyes off Gabe for a moment, and I deserve that. I messed up. But don't you dare accuse me of using our relationship as a means to slack off on my job. I am good at my job. In fact, I am *great* at my job, and you know it. What you just said to me, what you accused me of, was hurtful, cruel and unacceptable. I honestly didn't think you were capable of such cruelty, but I guess I was wrong." Her throat ached from holding back tears. "I was wrong about a lot." She sniffed, wiping the back of her wrist beneath her nose. She could cry more once she got in her car. But right now, she had to get it all off her chest. Say her piece, especially since she'd probably never see him again.

Pushing her chest out and shoulders back, she started at the back of his head, her chin up, her breathing steady.

"I might deserve to be fired, but you don't deserve me. Keep your money. I don't want it. Please tell Gabe that I'm sorry, and that I love him." A tear trickled down her cheek at the thought of never seeing that sweet little boy again and a sob clutched her chest causing her to choke. She had to get out of there.

She let out a shaky breath, but her heart felt just a fraction lighter. Unlike when she'd split up with Ken, this time she'd stood up for herself. This time she defended herself and put the man, the asshole in his place. And it felt good.

She stopped on the threshold that led out to the hallway and gave one last look at him, willing him to turn around and see that they were both at fault but could get past this. That they had something amazing and it wasn't worth ending it over a mistake. But he didn't. He didn't so much as flinch.

She gripped the doorjamb to steady herself, taking a deep breath she said what she'd hoped she'd never have to say, least of all to him. "Goodbye, Mark. And good luck." She stared at his back, his hands now clasped behind him, his body rigid, consumed with rage.

She swallowed down the hurt, the anger and the fear of the unknown and left. Only this time, she held her head high and she didn't look back.

# Chapter 14

Emmett blew out a breath before tipping his coffee up and taking a sip. "That's rough, bro."

Mark ran his fingers through his hair. He'd taken the last week off at work in order to deal with Gabe, and today was his first day back. He was exhausted. He hadn't found a new therapist or educational assistant, and Gabe's teacher was finding Gabe too difficult to manage at school without one-on-one support. He was acting out, being aggressive with other kids, hurting himself. It was like when Cheyenne had left all over again. Mark had kept Gabe home from school for a few days, meeting with Janice Sparks and discussing the dismissal of Tori.

Janice had been none too pleased with Mark and the fact that he'd fired Tori over her first offense, especially since her accomplishments far outweighed her one mishap. She encouraged him to reconsider and contact Tori, but he'd simply changed the subject.

"What are you going to do?" Will asked.

"I have no clue." Mark wished his coffee was Irish. He'd been hitting the bourbon hard the last few nights. It was the only thing that seemed to help him sleep. Not that he slept much or very well.

The three of them were sitting having coffee at the coffee shop across the street from the hospital. Emmett was done his shift, Will started in an hour, and Mark was on a break. It was a rarity that they all managed to get away at the same time during the day, but after Mark had abruptly taken time off from work, his buddies had rallied and insisted on coffee. Riley was off on paternity leave, as his wife, Daisy, had just had their second child.

"Have you heard from her?" Emmett asked.

Mark shook his head. "No, and I doubt I will. Not after the way I treated her, the things I said."

"You were angry," Will added. "She has to realize that."

"Would Amber be so understanding?" Mark asked. Will's wife, Amber, was a fiery redhead who was barely five feet tall if that. She ran her family's construction business and didn't take shit from anyone, particularly men.

Will's eyes bugged out. "Hell no. She would have told me to fuck right off. Or her new favorite saying, one she learned from our nieces, 'Sit on a fork and spin.'"

Emmett snorted. "Kids!"

Will shook his head. "Glad I'm just an uncle. I couldn't handle that shit every day."

"Ah, it's not so bad. Particularly if you get one as cute as mine," Emmett joked.

"Fine. Josie is an exception. I'd take your kid in a heartbeat. But only because she loves her Uncle Will so much. Says I'm cooler than her daddy."

Emmett bit into his Danish. "That's because you bought her fucking horseback riding lessons for her birthday."

Will's smile was devious, and he raised his paper cup in the air to toast himself. "Best gift ever. Give them an experience, but make the parents take them to it. Over and over and over again." His laugh grew the longer Emmett glared at him.

Emmett sobered and fixed his gaze on Mark. "Are you going to hire somebody else for Gabe?"

Mark exhaled, his eyes catching on something, more like *someone* across the road. Both men followed his eyes.

"Is it her?" Will asked, leaning forward and peering out the window.

Mark shook his head. "I thought it was. But that woman just has the same coat and hair color as Tori." She wasn't as beautiful as Tori, though. Couldn't hold a candle to her.

"Dude, you should go talk to her. Apologize. Explain that you overreacted," Emmett said. "She's a smart woman. She'll understand."

Mark made a noise in his throat. "This coming from the man who has given her the cold shoulder since day one."

Emmett made a face of remorse. "I'm sorry. You know I'm just looking out for you and Gabe. But I probably let my own shit and anger over Tiff and Huntley or whatever cloud my judgment and acceptance of Tori."

"Sure did," Mark said quietly.

Emmett's lip twisted. "Sorry."

Mark glanced at his watch. He had to be getting back to the hospital. He had an appointment with an oncology patient in twenty minutes. "I accused her of being lazy in her job because she was sleeping with me."

Will whistled and averted his eyes.

Emmett winced.

"I know I fucked up. She and that strong spine of hers made sure to tell me that before she slammed my front door."

"Who's with Gabe right now?" Emmett asked.

"My mother. But she can only handle him for so long. I'm going to have to head home early. The respite worker will come for a bit tomorrow and Saturday night so I can go to Liam's."

His friends nodded.

"Well, I'm off tomorrow," Emmett offered. "If you want me and Josie to pop by for a bit and watch him, we can."

Mark pushed out his chair and stood up. "Thanks." He tossed his cup into the recycling. "I've got to get back."

Will's hand shot out, and he stopped Mark from moving. "Dude, deny it all you want, but you love her."

Mark didn't say anything. Of course, he loved her. He'd given up denying it the moment he realized he'd lost her. He'd fallen hard for Tori. Then he'd gone and said things so unforgivable, the universe had probably deemed him unworthy of love for the rest of his life. Destined to live the rest of his days alone and miserable until it consumed him.

"I can see it on your face," Will went on. "If you love her, then fix this."

Mark leaned into the door to open it, shaking free of his friend's grasp. "How can she forgive me when I can't even forgive myself?"

"Retail therapy!" Isobel grinned from across the clothes rack. "Nothing quite like it."

Tori gave her sister a sardonic look. "Not like I can exactly *afford* to be spending my sorrows away. I'm jobless, remember?"

Isobel shrugged. "Then just try shit on. Or we can go halfers on something and share it." She winked at her sister. "It helps we're the same size."

"You still owe me my favorite cashmere sweater and black skinny jeans. I saw them in your latest Instagram post. I want them back."

"Just 'cause we're the same size doesn't mean you can pull off everything I can pull off. I really think that sweater looks better on me." Her smile was devious.

Tori grabbed a pair of gloves and playfully tossed them at her baby sister. "I want that sweater back."

"Yeah, but lilac is really more *my* color. You're more of a winter, and I'm an autumn." She pulled out a beautiful royal blue V-neck sweater. "*This* is more you. You should try it on."

Tori grabbed it from her and, before even looking at it, she turned over the price tag. She nearly had a stroke. "Not for eighty fucking dollars. I'd never wear the thing for fear of wrecking it."

Isobel rolled her eyes. "You're not going to be poor forever. Your luck is around the corner. I just know it."

Oh, how Tori wished she could be the eternal optimist like her baby sister. Iz really did see the best in everyone and every situation. Sometimes it got annoying ... like now.

"Can I have my dog walking business back?" she asked, putting the expensive sweater back on the rack.

Isobel made a face. "But I really like the puppies. Can't you just find new dogs? We could take them walking together. Have a puppy party." Her eyes lit up.

Tori slid her sister the side-eye. "I want my dogs back."

"Tori!"

She'd recognize that voice anywhere. She'd only heard it a few times, and when he'd used it, he'd been in a panic, but it still melted her heart that he loved her so much he said her name.

"Tori!"

She spun around to find Gabe running down the aisle toward her, an enormous smile on his face, arms flailing and running shoes making a loud slapping sound on the bright white tile.

He heaved himself into her arms. "Tori!"

Tori wrapped her arms around the little boy, burying her nose into his hair and squeezing him tight. She didn't think she'd ever see him again, let alone hug him.

"Aw, buddy. I've missed you. How've you been?"

He nuzzled into her neck, murmuring her name over and over again. She let herself close her eyes for just a moment. He wasn't hers. He never would be. Wouldn't even be a client again, but for just this moment, she allowed herself to find some joy. Because Gabe was pure joy. Footsteps behind them forced her to open her eyes.

"I wouldn't have believed it if I hadn't seen it for myself. He actually does say your name."

Her heart ached inside her chest, and she fought to temper her breathing.

"Hello." His deep voice shook her down to her very core.

Tori lifted her head, reluctantly letting Gabe go. "Hello."

Mark looked just as handsome as ever. Though maybe it was wishful thinking or projection or something, but the skin beneath his eyes seemed just a touch dark. Was he as distraught as she was? Had he been losing sleep too?

She shook that thought from her head before it had a chance to put down any roots. Of course he wasn't losing sleep over firing her. He'd probably already found a replacement for her, an intervention therapist a million times better.

Ken. Mark. They always found someone better than Tori.

"How have you been?" His words were forced and his gorgeous green eyes sad.

At least she thought they looked sad.

"I'm okay."

"Have you found a job?"

She nibbled on her bottom lip. Should she lie?

"No, not yet." She'd always been a crappy liar.

"But she has *many* interviews coming up. Lots of prospects," Isobel chimed in, sidling up next to her sister and looping a protective arm around Tori's shoulders. "Right, Tor?"

Tori simply swallowed.

Mark's gaze burned into her. "That's good. I'm happy for you."

The riot of emotions inside her was unsettling. She was angry with him for how he'd spoken to her, the things he'd said, the things he'd accused her of. But she was also so heartbroken, it pained her to look at him. Pained her to look at Gabe. She'd lost so much in the blink of an eye, it was worse than when Ken had kicked her out. A million times worse.

Her head tipped down and she stared at her feet, but that didn't last for long. Isobel elbowed her. "Don't you dare cower," she murmured. "He fucked up, too. At least you owned your screwup."

156

God, she loved her sister.

Tori lifted her head and narrowed her gaze at Mark, mustering up all the strength and courage she could find, right down to the tip of her pinky toe. She grabbed all of that confidence and bundled it up tight until it made her stand up as tall, straight and confident as she could.

Mark shifted uncomfortably on his feet.

Good, she was unnerving him.

He deserved to feel like shit.

He cleared his throat. "Well, uh, we should probably get a move on." He took Gabe's hand. "Come on, pal."

Gabe went to rip his hand away and at the same time lunged for Tori. "TORI!"

Mark's face fell. He didn't want to make a scene. "Come on, Gabe. Let's go."

"TORI!"

Emotion burned at the back of Tori's throat.

Mark grabbed Gabe around the waist. "I know, buddy. I know. But we have to go."

"TOOOOOOORI!" He kicked and punched, bowed his body and tried to wriggle away. Back to her. "Tooooori!"

People all over the department store stopped and stared at the histrionics. Mark's face was beet red, and tears streamed down Gabe's face as his father practically dragged him, kicking and screaming, across the floor toward the front door.

Hot tears pricked Tori's eyes as she watched it all unfold.

Just as they got to the door, Mark still battling it out with a determined and angry Gabe, Mark lifted his head up and his eyes met hers. Pain, regret, sadness. They were all there. Staring straight at her.

She felt all those things in her heart too. She'd fallen in love with him. In love with both of them. The empty hole inside her chest where Gabe and Mark had once been was now a wound so big, she wasn't sure it'd ever completely heal. She never should have let her personal life interfere with her work life. She should have told Ken to go away, rather than engage with him. Because look what it cost her. She'd regret that decision for the rest of her life. She'd regret Ken for the rest of her life.

"Let's go," Isobel said softly, urging Tori to turn around. "They're not yours anymore."

Nodding reluctantly, Tori turned around, only to hear one last long, low moan of her name as Mark pulled his sobbing son out into the parking lot and out of her life for good. "Toooooooooooooooorrrrriiiiiiiii!"

Her heart shattered.

# Chapter 15

♥

Tori sat down on her couch, tucking her legs beneath her. Mercedes, always a reliable friend when a relationship hit the fan, handed her a glass of wine and a plate with two slices of barbecue chicken pizza with pineapple and banana peppers.

Tori sipped her wine. "Thanks."

Mercedes sat down on the opposite end of the couch and bit into her vegetarian pizza. She groaned in delight, allowing her eyes to close and a smile to coast across her mouth as she continued to chew. Her long blonde hair was in a simple French braid down her back, and she was dressed down in worn jeans and a gray waffle-knit long-sleeve T-shirt. Mercedes worked in fashion, so she was usually dressed to impress, with impeccable makeup and chic clothing. It was nice to see her without any makeup and dressed casually like the rest of the world.

Tori was in her pajamas. She'd put them on as soon as she and Iz arrived home from shopping, her soul in a million pieces after running into Mark and Gabe and seeing Gabe react the way he did.

Mercedes opened her blue-gray eyes and pinned them on Tori. "Men are dumb. Particularly the hot, overly educated, super-fuckable ones."

Tori snorted.

Isobel raised her own wineglass in the air. "Cheers to that." She shook her head. "I hope Gabe sacked his dad in the nuts as he tried to get him into his car seat. Would serve him right."

Mercedes made a *mhmm* noise.

Tori frowned.

"I can't believe him." Mercedes tucked her feet beneath her like Tori. "You were obviously the best thing that happened to that little boy. Fucking Ken had to go and screw it all up."

Tori studied the pinot noir in her glass, swishing it around until it created "legs" or streams meandering down toward the bottom. A good wine had great legs. "Do you guys think I overthink relationships to the point of sabotaging them?"

"Yes," both women said in unison.

Tori's head snapped up, and she gaped at them. "Really?"

"I'm always telling you to stop overthinking things," Isobel said blandly. "Ken was the first guy that ever dumped you. And now Mark. Everyone was surprised, most of all me, when you agreed to marry Ken." She bit into her Greek pizza. Each woman had ordered her own medium-size pizza. They were in a gorging, not-sharing mood.

"Yeah, like, weren't you planning to break up with Ken, and then he popped the question?" Mercedes set her empty plate down on the coffee table, then grabbed a chenille throw off the back of the couch and draped it over her legs.

"She was," Isobel replied. "I thought she was calling me to tell me that she'd finally skidded Ken, only to be asked if I'd be her maid of honor."

"Because you said I overthink things and break up with guys all the time. So I went against my norm and looked for all the good in Ken. All the happiness he brought into my life. And when he asked me to marry him," she trailed off.

"I'm sorry," Isobel said. "I was wrong." She picked at a stray thread on her big chambray blanket scarf. "You were listening to your gut, and here I thought you were just being nitpicky. That you were just bored with the guys you were dating and breaking up with them because of something silly, like long nose hair or that they snored. Sometimes I can be too much of an optimist, and it can get in the way of seeing who people clearly are. Had I just let you dump Ken when you wanted to, none of this would have happened."

Tori leaned forward and put her hand on her sister's denim-clad thigh. "Don't change who you are, Iz. I love how positive and upbeat you are. You always see the good in people."

Isobel's pout morphed into a lip twist. Her eyes held so much sadness and remorse. "Even when there is no good to be seen."

"Like with Ken," Mercedes added.

Isobel nodded.

Tori held no animosity toward her sister for convincing her to stay with Ken. At the end of the day, it had been Tori's choice and no one else's. She had stayed with Ken. Decided to marry him. To halt her own aspirations for a higher education and career in exchange for Ken putting her through school later. What a joke that'd been. But none of it was Isobel's fault. None of it.

Tori's sister's empathy was not only her greatest attribute, but it was also one of her biggest weaknesses. Since the girls were small, Isobel had always been a bleeding heart. Most often this trait was harmless and sweet, like when she gave away her lunch every day at school for a year to the homeless woman and her dog that lived in the park beside the school. But then sometimes it was dangerous, such as the time she nearly got abducted when she agreed to go help a strange man find his lost puppy. It'd taken Tori grabbing her little sister's hand and telling the man to *fuck off* or she would call the police for the guy to leave them alone.

Tears welled up in Isobel's eyes. "I'm sorry, Tor. I know you loved Mark. Loved them both."

Emotion clawed at the back of Tori's head and deep in her throat. She'd shed enough tears over the last few days to last a lifetime. She thought she was cried out, yet here her body had more stores and was threatening to do it again.

Tori grabbed her sister's hand and hauled her over to the couch so she was between her and Mercedes. "I don't need a man in my life," she choked, wiping at her eyes. "Not when I have the best sister in the world." She placed a hand on Mercedes's shoulder. "And incredible friends who show up when I need them the most."

Mercedes's hand landed on top of Tori's, her smile wide. She raised her wineglass in the air. "To women. To sisters. To girlfriends. The only real people you can trust and depend on."

Tori and Isobel clinked their glasses with hers.

"To women."

"Dude," Scott scoffed, collecting all the cards and making them all face the same way so he could start shuffling. "That was low."

"Agreed," Adam grunted.

"Yep." Zak nodded.

"Way to punish the best thing that's happened to you in a long time." Everyone stopped chewing, drinking, shuffling and checking their phones to stare at Liam. He shrugged. "What? Just 'cause I'm a cynic and don't believe in love, doesn't mean I don't think ol' Marky Mark screwed the pooch on this one. That chick was the best thing to happen to him and Gabe in a long time, and he fucked it up."

Adam elbowed Mark. "Well, now that The Grinch has confirmed you're a royal fuckup, it's official. What are you going to do about it?"

Mark groaned and hung his head. He'd felt like shit all day. It had taken nearly an hour to get Gabe into the back of his SUV and buckle him in, then the kid had screamed and wailed in the backseat for the entire drive home. He'd even started chewing on his hand and hitting himself in the head, inflicting pain. It broke Mark's heart.

Wait, no. The look on Tori's face as she turned around and walked away from them had broken his heart. The sound of his son losing his mind after losing yet another person he'd grown close to had taken his broken heart and pulverized it into a million pieces.

Once home, Gabe had continued to throw a fit. It wasn't until Mark held him in his lap, squeezing him tight and applying deep pressure, humming Gabe's favorite song, that the little guy finally calmed down. Mark hated putting Gabe in a hold. Hated every goddamn minute of it. He managed to turn it into a hug, but he knew what it truly was. He'd taken nonviolent crisis intervention training at the recommendation of Gabe's behavioral consultant. It taught Mark how to put Gabe in a safe hold if need be. How to get out of a hair pull or a bite, how to deflect a hit or a kick without harming his child. So far, Gabe had never shown any real aggression or tried to attack Mark. But the hold did stop Gabe from trying to hurt himself, and it seemed to calm him down and bring him out of his fit faster than just letting it take its course.

When he'd finally calmed down, Gabe sat in his father's lap and cried himself to sleep. Only once he knew Gabe was asleep did Mark let his own tears fall. Tori really had been the best thing to happen to them. She understood Gabe. Loved him. He'd come leaps and bounds in his development in their short time together, and most of all—he was happy again. It'd been a long time since Mark had seen such happiness in his son. But every day he spent with Tori made his son shine brighter, smile bigger and love harder.

Mark was happy again too. When Tori was in their home, in his bed, in his arms, he felt whole again. He felt like he could take on the world because he had a good woman by his side, as his partner. They would tackle the shit life threw at them together and come out of the other side of the storm unscathed and stronger than ever.

And he'd gone and fucked it all up.

Fucked it up royally.

He'd fired her. Kicked her out of his home. Shamed her. Blamed her.

He wouldn't hold it against her if she never wanted to see his face again.

And yet, she'd been cordial to him this afternoon. After everything he said, the way he behaved, she was still the classiest woman he'd ever met. Held her head high, embraced his son and not made a scene. No, that scene had been made by Mark and Gabe.

He didn't blame Gabe. That was how his son showed his frustration. He didn't have words, didn't understand why Tori was no longer in his life, and so when he saw her again, he found hope. And Mark had snatched that hope right out of his son's hands.

"I feel like we're beating a dead horse here." Emmett's voice snapped Mark out of his thoughts. All the guys were staring at him around the table. "Will and I already told him to go to her and fix this."

Mark didn't say anything.

"You going to go to her?" Scott asked.

Mark shook his head. "She'll probably slam the door in my face."

Emmett tipped his beer up. "Maybe. Maybe not."

"No, she will. And I deserve it. I was horrible to her."

"Well, that's true. But you said she's mature and classy. She might just hear you out," Adam offered.

Tori was incredibly mature. And she was classy as fuck. But that didn't mean that the woman didn't have a limit. It didn't mean that all the class in the world would stop her from dismissing him, not hearing him out, not giving him another chance. He had the chance to apologize to her this afternoon at the store and he didn't. He should have begged for her forgiveness right then and there. Instead, he tore his kid away from her, gutting them all in the process.

She had every right to tell him to go to hell.

Too late. He was already there.

"Do you want her back?" Emmett asked, reading Mark's mind.

"I do."

"As Gabe's therapist?"

"As everything. I want *her*."

"Well, then, what the fuck are you still doing *here*?" Liam asked, shooting Mark a look that was a weird mix of irritation but also hope.

As much as he played up the love cynic, Liam really was a tremendous guy at the root of it all. It's why he'd started The Single Dads of Seattle to begin with. He wanted a safe place for men, fathers to come and talk, commiserate and find solace and comfort in a world that really didn't lend them much. He might not believe in love, but he believed in happiness.

Mark peeled at the label on his beer bottle. "She doesn't deserve me."

Atlas, the new guy, who had remained quiet until then, growled across the table.

Mark lifted his eyes to meet Atlas's.

"You're a dumb fuck."

Mark's eyes went wide.

"I don't know you. But what I've seen so far, you're a dumb fuck. A nice guy, but a dumb fuck. You didn't know how amazing you had it until you lost it, and now you're making up every excuse in the book to not go and win her back. If I could have one more day with my wife, I'd do anything and everything in my power to get it. Anything and everything for an hour, even a minute. If you've found someone that makes you feel like that, makes you feel like you can take on the storm, take on the world and not be swallowed up by it, fucking hold on to her, fucking fight for her. Be the man she deserves."

Liam hadn't said much about Atlas, just that he was a widower, worked with Liam at the law firm and had a young daughter named Aria. How his wife had died, Liam didn't say.

Atlas's bottom lip wobbled and his jaw tightened as raw emotion dashed across his face. "You go to her."

Mark swallowed.

A fist slammed on the table, making them all jump. Atlas's eyes grew fierce. "Get the fuck up and go! Now!" He choked out the last word, then stood, turned his head to hide his face, and stalked his big frame off to the kitchen.

All the other men at the table sat in silence.

Mark pushed himself up out of his seat, not saying a word. He grabbed his wallet, phone and left.

"Hey!" Liam called after him, Mark's hand poised on the door handle. Liam rested his hand on Mark's shoulder. "Things with Atlas are still pretty raw."

Mark nodded. "I kind of figured."

Liam's lips flattened out and he nodded solemnly. "He's actually a pretty fantastic guy, just intense and still hurting."

Mark glanced down the hallway toward the kitchen. "He's right, though. I am a dumb fuck. I fucked up big time."

Liam's smile was small but genuine, his dark eyes glowing from the pot lights overhead. "But unlike Atlas, you can get her back."

"Tell him I'm sorry."

"He'll be okay." He squeezed Mark's shoulder. "Go get her back."

Mark opened the door. "I'll let you know how it goes." He headed out into the night toward his car.

"And I'll give you a discount on your next divorce!" Liam called after him.

Mark raised his hand in the air and flipped Liam the bird, all to the loud laughter of his friend.

Mark pulled up to Tori's townhouse. The moment he turned off the ignition, fear ratcheted up his spine.

He couldn't lose her.

Atlas's words came back at him. "Be the man she deserves."

A ripple of light from inside the house drew his eyes up from where he'd been staring at the steering wheel. A figure, beautiful as ever, stood in the living room window peering out at him. All he could see was her silhouette, but even that was stunning.

*Get the fuck up and go! Now!*

Well, at least now she knew he was here. If she opened the door, that was a good sign, right?

*Be the man she deserves. Win her back. Fight for her.*

He got out of his car and stalked up the driveway to the front door, his eyes glued to her in the window. He couldn't see her face, but her posture changed. Her back went ramrod straight, then she was gone.

He was just reaching the landing when the door swung open.

"What the hell do you want?"

He recognized that voice, but the way the light from inside poured into the night, he couldn't tell who it was.

He climbed the stairs.

It was Mercedes. He recognized her from the night he met Tori, only she had far less makeup on, was in jeans and a T-shirt and seemed a lot less drunk and a lot more pissed off.

"I've come to talk to Tori," he said, trying to peer behind Mercedes, but she spread her arms across the doorjamb and moved her head whichever way he moved his.

"She doesn't want to see you," she snapped. "She's had her heart broken enough times in the last year."

Mark's gut twisted.

The woman from the department store earlier in the day appeared behind Mercedes. She looked enough like Tori, with her porcelain skin, button nose and high cheekbones, that he was certain this was her sister Isobel.

"What do you want to say to her?" Isobel asked.

"I want to talk to *Tori*," he said. "I want to see her."

Footsteps behind the other two women drew their attention, and they parted on either side of the door to let her through. Just like that first night when he'd shown up on her doorstep, slightly drunk and wanting to talk about their

167

mistake in his kitchen, she looked incredible. Rosy complexion, fresh from the shower, hair piled up high on her head, pajama pants and a tight white tank top. Her nipples pebbled when the cool winter air hit her.

She must have noticed where his gaze landed, because with an eye roll, she crossed her arms in front of her chest. "What are you doing here?"

But unlike that first time, he wasn't there to tell her they made a mistake. He was there to get her back, to tell her that *he* had made the mistake—and many of them. He made the mistake of firing her and speaking to her the way he did, shaming her, blaming her, accusing her. Up until then, every decision he'd made with regards to Tori had been the right one, though. From intruding on her divorce party, to hiring her, kissing her on her birthday, bringing her into his bed and falling in love with her, every decision had been right. Everything in his life had been right since meeting Tori. And now he'd gone and fucked it all up.

"Hmm?" she probed, cocking her hip out. Her expression was curious as her gaze slowly ran over his face. No sadness. No anger. But he could see the questions. The wondering. "What are you doing here?"

"I'm a dumb fuck."

Her lips pursed. "Not going to argue with you."

A laugh rumbled in his chest. Fuck, he loved her.

"I messed up. Big time. I never should have fired you. Never should have spoken to you, treated you the way I did. I was wrong. None of what I said was true. Not a word. I'm so sorry."

Something flashed behind her eyes, and they softened just a touch, but she was still heavily guarded. And rightfully so. He'd broken her heart. She'd only just started to glue the pieces of her life, of her heart back together after her separation, and Mark had gone and taken a sledgehammer to it all, and all before the glue had even dried.

She was waiting for him to continue.

"I want you back."

One eyebrow lifted a fraction of an inch.

"I need you back."

"For Gabe."

"Yes."

Color stained her cheeks. Even wearing a frown, she was positively gorgeous. Her eyes were a smoldering blue fire, boring into his soul. "I see. So you need me to come back and work for you."

He nodded. "Yes. Gabe needs you. He's regressing, having more behaviors than ever. You saw him at the department store today."

"I did, yes."

What was going on? Why was she being so reserved? So distant?

"So, you need me back for Gabe? Just Gabe?"

Fuck, he was a dumb fuck.

He pushed his way inside, elbowing her sister and Mercedes out of the way. They took the hint and retreated to the living room. He boxed Tori against the wall. Her gaze flew up to his face and she studied him, her body still steeled against his attentions. She was protecting her heart. There was a twelve-inch-thick concrete wall around it, twenty feet high and barbed at the top. She wasn't letting just anybody in anymore. He'd have to earn her love again.

And he would.

"I love your son, Mark. But I can't come back and work for you if all you want is an employee. I can't. It would just be too difficult. Eventually you'll start dating again and ..." She drifted off, unable to look him in the eye. Emotion made her throat undulate on a hard swallow. "I just couldn't watch ... I've fallen in love with you. As hard as I tried not to. As hard as I tried to keep it light and fun and just the two of us enjoying each other's bodies, each other's company, it turned into more. I couldn't watch you start a life with someone else while I sat on the sidelines and worked with Gabe. It would kill me."

Resting his elbows on the wall next to her head, he smoothed the stray tendrils of her hair off her face, cupping the perfect heart-shape in his hands. "*I* want you. I want you in my life. My house. My bed. My arms ... my heart. I need you. Gabe needs you. I need you to come back to us. If more children is what you want, then we can discuss it. Or we could adopt. If marriage is what you want, then I want that too. I want *you,* and I'll do whatever I have to to get you back."

Finally, she let one of the building blocks tumble down from atop her wall. Her bottom lip trembled, and a tear slipped down her flushed cheek. Not releasing her head, he moved his thumb and wiped away the tear. Her long, feathered lashes were spiked from her tears and fluttered as she finally looked up into his eyes.

"God, you're beautiful," he murmured. "You have the most intense blue eyes I've ever seen."

She leaned into his palm and shut her eyes once more for half a second.

"I'm sorry I brought my personal life, my personal problems to work. It will never happen again."

No. She hadn't done anything wrong. He was the one who had fucked up. And Ken, that motherfucker. He'd deal with him soon enough.

"Look at me," he ordered.

Her gaze speared him.

"You did nothing wrong. *Nothing.* You hear me? I overreacted. Out of fear for Gabe. Jealousy that you'd seen your ex. Jealousy and anger that your asshole of an ex had been around my child."

Her luscious lips dipped into a pout.

"But it was mostly fear." He exhaled, shutting his own eyes for a moment, then glancing down at his feet. "Gabe is my life. And the thought of something happening to him. Of losing him ..."

A small, delicate hand landed on his chest.

"I was afraid. And I let that manifest into anger, and I reacted irrationally. I said some horrible things to you, things I take back, things I never meant. Not for one second." His eyes met hers. "Tori, I am so sorry. Please, give me another chance to prove to you how much you mean to me. To *us.* We need you." He pressed his forehead to hers. "I need you."

Her fingers bunched in the front of his shirt.

His lips brushed against hers. "I love you."

# Chapter 16

♥

Mark followed Tori into the living room. Her hand felt good in his. Right.

She glanced at her sister and Mercedes, who sat on the couch with death-stares directed right at Mark. "Can you guys give us some time? I know it was girls' night, but ..."

Both women nodded, shooting Mark even more daggers, as they pried themselves off the couch, taking their wineglasses with them.

"We'll just be upstairs," Mercedes said, pointing two fingers at Mark, then at her eyes, then back at Mark to let him know she was watching him.

Tori's lips twisted. "No, I mean, can you guys go?"

"You're sure?" Isobel asked. It appeared as though she and her sister were having a wordless conversation. Their lips never moved, but their eyes said a thousand things.

"I'm sure," Tori said softly. "We'll be okay."

Grumbles from her protectors, followed by the chugging of wineglasses, the closing of pizza boxes and finally the slamming of the front door, suddenly left them in a deafening silence.

Mark stood beside Tori in the living room, their hands still clasped.

But not for long. She released his hand and went over to sit in the chair. He made note that she didn't sit on the couch, which would have invited him to sit next to her.

"We have some things to work out before we move forward," she said, nodding at the couch. "You can't just tell me you love me and expect things to go back to how they were."

Oh, if life were only that simple.

Her stunning blue eyes pinned on him. "Sit."

He sat.

"Now, I realize I fucked up, bringing my personal problems into my professional life, but it was a one-off, and I have apologized repeatedly for it."

Between now and just moments ago at the front door, her spine had grown tenfold. He loved it. He loved a woman who didn't take shit and stood up for herself, even to him.

He nodded. "I know it was. I know you have. But you didn't fuck up. Ken showing up wasn't your fault. I know that now. You need not apologize again. There's nothing to apologize for."

New conviction burned in her eyes. "Fine. But you also can't just show up on my doorstep and expect me to forgive you simply because you uttered three little words. You hurt me, Mark. You shamed me. Made it out that because we were sleeping together, I grew complacent in my job, in Gabe's care."

Bile burned the back of his throat. If he could go back in time, take it all back, he would. Every last word. He would handle all of it so differently.

"If anything, because I cared about you, I cared more about Gabe. I took my job more seriously because I didn't want to fuck up all the amazing things that were finally happening to me. All the things that finally brought me joy again." She grabbed her wineglass but didn't take a sip. Instead, she just stared down into it. "It's been a while since I've found any kind of joy."

"It'll be different this time. I swear. We'll be upfront and open about our relationship with everyone. With Gabe, with his teachers, with Janice Sparks. With whoever you want. You want me to meet your parents? Done. Let's go next weekend. You want to meet mine? Totally, we can have them over for dinner on Friday."

She shook her head. "You're saying all the right things ..."

Mark fell to his knees on the floor, shuffling over to stand in front of her. "What can I do to *show* you I mean it? To truly earn your forgiveness? To let you know that I'm a dumb fuck who let the best thing that had ever happened to him and his kid slip away?"

"Stand up," she said with an eye roll.

He didn't stand but instead perched on the end of the coffee table, their knees close but not touching. "What can I do, Tori? You want me to grovel?"

"No. I don't want you to grovel. I believe that you mean it. That you're sorry for how you treated me. And I do forgive you."

Relief swamped him.

"I just want to discuss where we're going to go from here."

He reached for her hands. Thankfully, she let him take them, lacing their fingers together. "We can go wherever you want to go. Gabe is lost without you." He kissed her knuckles. "So am I."

"I want to work with Gabe again, but I can't let you pay for my schooling. That just feels like too much. Even if we're going to be together, I'm also on the quest for my independence, remember? You need to let me keep working at that."

"You want me to keep paying you for his therapy though, right?" He couldn't let her do it for free, never. He'd figure out some other way to get money to her if she refused his payment.

She nodded. Thank God. "Yeah, I mean I still need to make a living. But I'll pay for my own schooling. I think maybe a contract might be a good idea. Do you think Liam could draw us up one?"

"A work contract? We have one."

"A *relationship* contract."

His lips twisted. "You want to know my hard limits?" She'd served him that opportunity on a silver platter. How could he not bite?

Tori rolled her eyes. "Yeah, sure. We can stay together as long as you're cool with pegging. This relationship needs to be equal on *all* levels. If I take it, so should you."

He dropped her hands, and his jaw dropped. His asshole, on the other hand, puckered up tighter than a nun's.

She tossed her head back and laughed. "Gotcha!"

Mark wiped his brow. "*Phew*. For a minute there I thought I was about to have a heart attack."

Shaking her head, she took his hands in hers again, massaging the backs with her thumbs. "But I do think a contract might be a good idea. Just so the muddy water we're already knee deep in doesn't turn into quicksand. We've gone beyond conflict of interest, and I'm now sleeping with my boss, in love with my boss and in love with his son. It's a complicated web we've gotten ourselves tangled up in."

He scooped her up from the chair, took her seat and plopped her on his lap. He was tired of not having her in his arms. She didn't fight him. He pressed a kiss to her forehead. "I'll talk to Liam."

"Thank you."

"Can I talk to Liam about something else too?"

She closed her eyes and leaned her head against his. "Hmm?"

"Your divorce. I'd like to help you out … financially and emotionally. Be whatever you need to rid him from your life for good. From *our* lives for good."

"*Our* lives …" She opened her eyes and looked down at him, her lips twisted into an amused grin.

"Yes. *Our* lives. Because it's not just you anymore. You don't have to weather this storm alone. You don't have to take on the monsters by yourself. I'm here every step of the way. I want to be your shoulder to cry on, your cheering squad and your rock. I want to be yours."

"Mine."

"For as long as you'll have me."

She scrunched up her face and turned away from him in thought. "Hmmm

... I'm going to have to think on that. This might just be a fling."

With a growl, he cupped her butt and powered them both up and out of the chair, falling on top of her on the couch. "Fling my incredibly puckered asshole," he said into her neck. "It's still terrified by that pegging comment a moment ago."

Her laugh made his shoulders relax and his heart swell. She poked a finger between the crease of his ass through his jeans. "You're not even a touch curious?"

Her giggle was infectious. His hand snaked up the hem of her tank top, and he cupped her breast. "Not even the slightest. Though I am curious about what your nipples taste like. It's been fucking ages." He shook like a junkie coming down from a high. "I'm going through withdrawals." He fished a breast out of her bra and latched onto a nipple, sucking hard until it peaked inside his mouth, and she gasped and arched her back.

Her hands threaded their way into his hair, and her fingers tugged until a dull but satisfying ache careened down his scalp and into his neck.

"Things are going to be different this time," he murmured, switching to the other breast. "I won't fuck up like I did before."

"You'll fuck up in different ways?"

He pinched her nipple. She yelped.

"Yes, I probably will. But I'll need you to keep loving me anyway, just like I'll keep loving you when you mess up."

"Oh, I never mess up."

He pinched her again. "Well, if you ever do, know I'll never treat you the way I did before. Never speak to you like that ever again. I'll keep loving you even through the hard stuff, even through the roadblocks and the storms."

Her lips fell to the top of his head. "Thank you."

He was about to take her top off completely when a knock at the door had them both pausing.

"Do you think your sister or Mercedes forgot something?" he asked, leaning up on one elbow and gazing down at her.

Her eyes were bright, and her face held a beautiful pink flush. She shook her head. "I don't think so. Unless it was a forgotten phone, they'd both know to not come back until tomorrow."

He sat up so she could adjust her top and stand up. He followed her to the door. "It's really fucking late. Who do you think it could be?" Tori peered through the peephole just as Mark pulled back the drapes of the big front window. "I don't see a car."

"That's because the motherfucker probably parked on the street," she said, turning to face him. Fury now replaced the happiness that had just moments ago filled her eyes. "It's Ken."

Oh, hell no.

Mark gently pushed her out of the way and opened the door. "What the fuck do you want?"

The look on the fucker's face was priceless. He hadn't been expecting Mark to open the door. Probably because his car wasn't there. He'd been hoping to catch Tori alone. Had he waited until Isobel and Mercedes left? Mark wouldn't put it past him. The man was pure trash.

But Ken recovered quickly, and his mouth went from a surprised *O* to a sinister sneer. "I'm here to speak to Tori."

"She's unavailable right now."

"Yeah? Too busy wiping your cum—"

"I'm going to stop you right there, pal." Mark's fists bunched at his sides. It was all he could do not to haul off and knock the guy clear into next week. "What do you want? Because from now on you can deal with me or Tori's lawyer, Liam Dixon, but you are no longer allowed to speak to or see Tori for any reason."

Ken snorted. "She's got you fighting her battles now, does she?"

"So what if she does? She's capable of fighting them on her own, but now she doesn't have to. She has me. We're a team."

So far, Tori had remained hidden behind the door. Ken didn't deserve to see her. Didn't deserve to share the same space or air with such a strong, amazing woman. Mark did feel her hand on his back, though, felt her strength pouring into him.

"I want my engagement ring back," Ken said haughtily.

Mark pinched his chin and tilted his head, squinting and making sure he looked down on Ken. He was a few inches taller than the weasel, but he wanted the man to think Mark towered over him. "Seems to me you *gave* her the engagement ring, and now it's hers."

"And the marriage is over. So it's mine now."

"Let's let the lawyers decide that, shall we?"

"She hit me! Did she tell you that? I could press charges for assault."

Mark began to close the door. He'd had more than enough of this douche to last a lifetime. "And your only witness to corroborate that claim is the five-year-old nonverbal autistic child you couldn't be bothered to help Tori find after he ran away because of your rage issues. I'm sure the courts are going to *love* this story. Come at us, man. Come at us with your guns blazing, because we're ready for you." He closed the door even more. Ken's hand landed on the side, and he tried to push it open. Mark leaned in close to the man's ear. "If you ever touch her again, I will make sure you don't have a pot to piss in when we're through with you. I will *destroy* you. You hear me?"

Ken's gulp was so loud, Mark was sure Tori heard it too.

But the man wasn't going to go down without a fight. Ken pushed harder on the door. "I know you two are sleeping together. I could report you. It's a conflict of interest."

Report them to whom?

The man was a fucking tool.

Mark rolled his eyes and shrugged, feigning indifference. Meanwhile, inside he was a volcano ready to erupt. "Go ahead, man. You fucked your hygienist. I'm not going to stand here and have a pissing match with you. So go away. Get a lawyer. Have a good night and don't forget to go fuck yourself." Then he slammed the door in Ken's face, plastered his back against it and let out a long exhale.

Tori's big blue eyes blinked up at him. "I'm sorry."

"Holy fuck. How did you stay married to that monster for so long?"

Her hand landed on his chest, and she stepped between his legs. "I have no idea. I drank the Kool-Aid."

"Kool-Aid is *really* bad for you." He cupped her butt.

"I know that now." Her hands on his chest softened into a gentle caress, and she slowly peppered warm kisses up his neck. "I much prefer a malbec, aged, refined, *mature*. Something I can sip and savor, swirl around on my tongue and let slide silkily down my throat."

Mark groaned as her hand maneuvered between them and she cupped his growing erection. "I have *a lot* of malbec at home."

"Enough to keep me satisfied?" She hummed against his neck.

"Enough to keep you satisfied for a lifetime."

She lifted her head and smiled, her eyes once again full of hope and joy. He never wanted to see them look any other way. "I think I can live with that."

Then he took her mouth with the same intensity and possessiveness that she took his heart: fierce, true and for fucking forever.

# *Epilogue*

*One year later ...*

"Everything seems to be in order," Liam said, sliding the document across the desk toward Tori. "Sign on the dotted line, and you are officially divorced. Mr. Snider will no longer be your husband. You will be *free*." He grabbed a pen from the square wooden pen box on his desk and handed it to her.

Tori took the pen from him and looked down at the divorce papers.

*Free.*

Free from Ken.

Mark reached for her left hand and laced his fingers through hers. "You okay?"

A small smile crept onto her face as she positioned the pen on the paper and signed her name. She dated it. Initialed where Liam had highlighted and then passed the papers back to her attorney. Only then did she turn to face Mark. "Never better."

Liam picked up the papers and tapped them on his glass-top desk twice to realign them. "Excellent. It's such a wonderful feeling, isn't it? To finally be rid of something so toxic in your life."

"Dude," Mark warned.

Liam threw his hands up in the air. "What? I'm just asking if she feels as good as I felt when I signed my divorce papers."

Tori's eyes focused on Liam for a moment and then Mark. "It does feel wonderful. I thought it would be a melancholy thing, but I really do feel free. The man was pure poison, and the way he's tried to paint me as the bad guy this whole time just proves it."

"I can't believe he made it drag out so long," Mark said, shaking his head. "Over a year of this bullshit."

Liam spun around in his chair and bent over, only to pop back up holding a bottle of prosecco and three flutes. "Bullshit's over and done with. Shall we celebrate?"

"Do you do this for all your clients?" Tori asked.

"Only the ones I like," he said with a grin before deploying the cork. "And only when I win big. Your ex hired a moron of an attorney. They had zero leg to stand on, and now Ken's going to be out even more money in legal fees. He should have just accepted our offer to settle in the first place and not taken us to court."

"I don't know what I ever saw in him," Tori said. She thanked Liam for her flute of bubbly.

"We all make mistakes," Liam said. "Lucky for you, you hired the right lawyer to help you fix those mistakes."

"You're not modest at all." Mark chuckled.

"Don't have to be when I'm this good."

Mark rolled his eyes.

"A toast?" Liam asked, lifting his glass.

Tori nodded. "To ... fixing our mistakes?"

"To kick-ass lawyers?" Liam suggested.

Tori laughed.

"How about ... to new beginnings," Mark offered.

Tori pinned her gaze on him, a small, knowing smile spreading across her face. "I love it."

"And I love you," he said, leaning forward and kissing her on the cheek.

"I like it." Liam pushed his flute higher into the air. "To new beginnings."

"To new beginnings," Tori and Mark said together.

They all clinked glasses, smiling and laughing as they sipped the chilled and delicious prosecco.

"So, what are your plans for the rest of the day ... for the rest of your lives?" Liam asked, leaning back in his high-back leather chair and resting his feet on the top of his file cabinet. He looked like he should have a cigar in his other hand or, at the very least, a pipe.

"Having a barbecue at the house this afternoon," Mark said. "A little impromptu, but you're welcome to pop by. I invited the guys and all the kids. Tori's family is going to be there, my parents too."

Something passed between the two men, but it disappeared before Tori could decipher their wordless man-conversation.

What was up?

"Sounds good. I'll bring Jordie. He's just with my parents for a few hours, but he loves Gabe, so he'll be excited to see him."

Tori and Mark both finished their wine, put their glasses on Liam's desk and stood.

Mark extended his hand over the desk and shook Liam's hand. "Thanks so much, dude. We really appreciate you helping Tori out like this. Helping *us* out. Means a lot."

Liam was all smiles. "Anytime. I'm glad we could drag another cheating scumbag through the mud."

Tori winced. Liam really was jaded.

Mark chuckled, though Tori could tell he was forcing it. "All right. We'll see you later?"

Liam's head bobbed, his dark brown eyes full of mischief like they always were. "Count on it." He wandered out from behind his desk, and he and Tori quickly embraced.

She pecked him on the cheek. "Thank you, Liam ... for everything."

This time his smile was far less cocky and mischievous. His eyes darted back and forth between Mark and Tori. Mark's hand was on the small of her back, and she leaned affectionately into him. Something almost akin to longing passed across Liam's face before he spoke. "I'm glad I could help. We all deserve to be happy. And if you two make each other happy, then I'm happy ... and rich." The cocky smile was back.

Mark shook his head with a laugh. "Send the invoice to my accountant." Pressure from his hand on Tori's back made her turn with him to leave.

"My secretary already sent it an hour ago," Liam called back, as Mark and Tori made their way down the hallway toward the front doors.

A few hours later, Mark and Tori's house was filled with people. Yes, it was Tori's house too. He wanted her in his life every day, all day, and every night, all night. Gabe had transitioned to Tori living with them more easily than any of them could have thought, and he was doing better than ever with his programs. He even started signing the word *dad* and was trying to say *Dad* but it came out more like "Da."

As much as Tori had to endure hellish moments in the last year, having a good woman in his life once again was like a dream for Mark. He finally had a woman who loved him and his son implicitly. And they loved her in return.

Mark had wanted Tori to move in with him as soon as she'd finished her house-sitting gig, but she'd refused. Something that equal parts frustrated him and made him have the utmost respect for her.

Her independence was paramount, and she didn't think she would have it moving in with Mark so soon after her separation with Ken. She and Isobel found a place together, and for eight months Tori lived on her own with her sister. She also enrolled in an online business management class that she paid for with money she earned from her photography side-business. During the week, she worked for Mark, and on the weekends they dated. All as per their relationship and work agreement.

But when the online course was finished, she agreed to move in with him, making Mark a very happy man because he finally had the woman he loved living with him. He finally had her in his life, his bed, and his arms. So even though she was up at night fretting about her divorce, he was right there next to her, holding her hand, wiping her tears and letting her know that everything would be okay. Because it would be. They were together, they loved each other, and he was going to take care of her, help her achieve her goals no matter what.

Liam had worked his magic, and now they were free. Free of Ken and his poisonous influence over their lives, free to truly enjoy their new life together, free to find their new beginning.

And that's just what Mark planned to do.

"Can I have everyone's attention, please?" Mark asked, using his big, stern doctor voice. The voice he generally reserved for when he'd reached his last nerve with Gabe or was tired of a resident or intern lipping it up to their attending.

Murmurs around the big back yard slowly came to a halt, and all eyes focused on Mark. Tori was across the grass chatting with her mother and sister. She quirked an eyebrow at him. Her mesmerizing blue eyes focused on him and only him.

Gabe was standing next to Mark, bouncing up and down in excitement. He had a box in his hand, and when Mark gave the all clear, Gabe knew what he had to do.

Mark waited a few more moments until everyone was quiet. Then he tapped Gabe on the shoulder.

The little boy leapt up into the air, then beelined it straight for Tori. She crouched down and welcomed him into her arms. He went willingly.

Mark began to walk slowly toward them.

"Victoria Mae Jones," he began. She released Gabe, stood up again and watched Mark approach her. All eyes were on them, but she only had eyes for him.

Mark only saw Tori.

Tori and Gabe.

His family.

His future.

"Victoria Mae Jones," he repeated. "You came into our lives at the perfect time. Brought back the light and chased away the darkness. Gabe loves you. I love you, and we couldn't imagine our world, our home, our lives or hearts without you."

Gabe handed her the box. She took it from him just as Mark reached them. He got down on one knee.

Gasps echoed around the yard.

Gabe went to his father and stood next to him until Mark tugged on his arm, then the little boy dropped to one knee as well. They'd rehearsed this close to one hundred times over the last few weeks. Gabe was doing great.

"Victoria, Tori ... *our* Tori, I know your marriage to one man just ended, but ... will you marry us?"

Tori's mouth opened, but no words came out.

Gabe stepped forward and grabbed the box from her, holding it up and encouraging her to take it again. To open it.

With a soft chuckle, she took it from him, her eyes full of love when she looked at Mark's son. She opened the box, and her eyes went wide.

Isobel and Mercedes had helped him pick out the ring.

Gabe bounded back to stand next to Mark, his hands flapping at his sides. Mark grabbed his son's hand and squeezed it. Now all they needed was Tori's hand, and their family would be complete.

She was still staring at the ring.

"Toori!" Gabe said, jumping on the spot, shaking his head and hands. "Toooooori!" He was all smiles as he flung himself back into her arms, nearly knocking her off her feet.

She caught him, her eyes finally lifting up from the ring box to find Mark. The unshed tears made the sapphire blue sparkle.

"We don't have to do it right away. We can wait a while, six months, a year. Whatever you need. I just need you to know that we want you forever."

A tear bolted down her cheek, but she was all smiles.

"Well?" Mark probed. "What do you say? You feel like making the day, the week, the month, the year, the life of a couple of guys who love you?"

She took the half step there was between them and reached for his hand, helping him rise to his feet. Gabe clung to both their legs, bouncing up and down and humming.

Her arms floated up and rested on his shoulders. "Nothing would make me happier."

Mark's grin hurt his face.

He pulled her arm down from off his shoulder and grabbed the ring box from her hand, opening it again and taking out the ring. She held out her finger, and he slipped it on.

It fit perfectly.

Just like she fit perfectly into Mark and Gabe's world.

"I love it," she whispered.

"And we love you," he said, wrapping his arms around her waist, lifting her up and spinning her around, all to the cheering and clapping of their friends and family.

When he put her back down on her feet, he hinged forward and scooped up Gabe, settling his son on his hip.

Tori wrapped her arm around Mark's waist, leaning in to peck Gabe on the cheek. "You did great, buddy."

Gabe was all smiles.

Mark bent his head and took Tori's mouth, pulling her tight to his chest and encouraging her to open for him. She did. He didn't care that his parents, her parents and all their family and friends were there. He loved this woman, and she had just agreed to be his wife. He was over the moon and not afraid to show it.

When they finally came up for air, Tori's eyes were bright and her cheeks a sexy pink. She licked her lips, gazing up at him with a look so filled with love and hope for the future, it winded him.

"To new beginnings?" she asked.

"To new beginnings." Then he kissed her again, because he could, and he would, every day for the rest of his life.

If you've enjoyed this book, please consider leaving a review wherever you purchased it. It really does make a difference and helps an independent author like me.

Thank you again.

Xoxo

Whitley Cox

## Chapter 1

"Can I wear my princess dress to dance class? And my tiara? And my cape? And my light-up princess shoes? Can I bring my magic wand? My fairy wings?"

Adam Eastwood had to stifle a chuckle at the excitement of his four-year-old daughter, Mira. "I don't think so, sweetheart. It says here that dancers are expected to wear tights, bodysuits and leather ballet or jazz shoes."

"What about a tutu?"

"It says a small ballet skirt is optional." He grabbed his phone and brought up the registration email that had shown up in his inbox last week.

Mira abandoned her dress-up box and came to sit next to him on the couch, immediately running her small hand over his short-trimmed beard. It was one of her favorite things to do. A sense of comfort for her. After her mother moved out, Mira had fallen asleep every night stroking her father's beard. Truth be told, it'd become a sense of comfort for him too.

"See, baby. It says here *no princess dresses or costumes*. Because they're worried about you not being able to move enough in the dresses or they might get wrecked."

Her big blue eyes, with long lashes, blinked a few times as she stared at the email from Benson School of Dance. She made an adorable pouty face but finally nodded. "Not even my tiara?"

She couldn't read, so he pointed at the address. "Says right here, no tiaras. Same reason as the costumes. What if it fell off and someone stepped on it? Cracked it?"

"I would be sad."

"That's right. So let's just stick with the new dance outfit we bought you yesterday, okay?"

Her sigh was big. His daughter was quite melodramatic when she wanted to be. "Okay."

He kissed her on the side of her head, her dark hair like watermelon-scented silk beneath his lips. "That's a good girl. Now go get changed. Dance class starts in half an hour."

She slid off the couch and skipped down the hallway. "Can I at least wear my princess underwear?"

Adam nodded his head and laughed. "Sure, honey. Go for it." He pushed himself up on the couch and wandered into the kitchen to prepare his daughter a snack for after dance.

It was only a one-hour class, and he would probably stick around, at least for the first class. But if swimming lessons and her small bout in gymnastics had taught him anything, it was even the smallest amount of play or exercise made his picky eater of a child *starving*.

"Pack my water bottle, Daddy," Mira called from down the hall. "And a grolla bar. The one with the chocolate chips."

Adam rolled his eyes. She knew what she wanted, he had to give her that. She just went about getting it in a very dictatorial way.

"She's going to be a leader," his grandmother would say. "A titan of industry."

"Or she's going to take over a nation and enslave the locals," his grandfather would add.

His grandmother would just chuckle, then scoop Mira up in her arms and plunk her on her lap, nuzzling her hair. "Our tiny Napoleon."

Mira's heavy-footed run echoed down the hallway as she ran her long-legged body toward him. She was tall for her age but all limbs. A bit gangly, but hopefully she would grow out of that. "Can you help me with my straps, Daddy? They're twisted." She made a face to describe what she meant, twisting her lips and wrinkling her nose.

He bent down and untwisted the straps of her bodysuit, then grabbed her skirt from her hands and helped her step into it. "Almost ready to go?"

She was all smiles. "Yep. I just need to get my ballet slippers."

"Okay, well, be quick about it. We don't want to be late on your first day."

She was already halfway down the hall. "Okaaaaay!"

Violet Benson took a deep breath and smoothed the black spandex of her ballet skirt down her legs.

It was opening day. A beautiful day. The sun was shining. The birds were singing. It was the first day of May, and Benson School of Dance was officially open to the public for dance lessons.

Her dream ... *their* dream was finally becoming a reality.

And she felt sick to her stomach.

"It'll be okay," her receptionist Kathleen cooed, her fingers tapping away on the keyboard. "You've created a beautiful studio. Everyone is going to love it. They're going to love you."

Violet swallowed. "I hope so."

She straightened the picture of Jean-Phillipe that didn't need to be straightened. His smile made the strings of her heart tighten. This had been his dream. And then it became their dream. Now it was her dream, and she was finally, after far too long, making it a reality.

"He's already so proud of you," Kathleen said, watching Violet run her finger over Jean-Phillipe's cheek. "You're going to do amazing things, put on amazing shows, and he'll be there for everything. Watching you, cheering for you."

Violet smiled at Kathleen, though it was a forced smile and one that she neither felt in her heart nor had the strength to keep on her face for more than a second or two. "It should be the both of us welcoming in our first students."

Kathleen stood up and wandered around to stand next to Violet, wrapping a motherly arm around her shoulder. "And it will be. He's here in spirit, and you're here in person."

The bell for the front door chimed, and the sound of parents and children filled the space.

Show time.

"Welcome, boys and girls, parents, grandparents. I am Miss Violet, your dance instructor, and I am so excited that you've all decided to try Benson School of Dance."

Ten children, all between the ages of four and six, sat on the floor at her feet. Their parents sat in chairs along the wall. Big eyes stared up at her. Hopeful eyes.

"How many of you have ever taken dance before?"

A few hands shot up.

"Parents? Do we have any dancing parents?"

One or two of the mothers waved their hands.

And the only father.

Hmm.

"So we've got some experienced dancers in our mix, as well as some beginners. That's wonderful. We welcome all levels."

One little girl, with the lilac bodysuit and skirt to match, put her hand in the air.

"Yes? What's your name, sweetheart?"

She stood up, confidence radiating from every part of her. "My name is Mira."

"Pleased to meet you, Mira. And how old are you?"

Mira held up four fingers. "I'm four and a half."

Violet grinned, chuckling to herself. "Four is a great age."

Mira nodded. "And a half."

"Right! That half is *very* important. Did you have a question, Mira?"

She nodded again. "Do you not let us wear tiaras because you're worried it will fall off our heads and someone will step on it and break it?"

A muffled laugh came over from the parents along the wall. The man who'd raised his hand, a very attractive man with blue eyes, coppery brown hair and a short-trimmed beard, was trying not to laugh but doing a terrible job of it. His big, muscular frame shook in his navy polo and worn jeans.

Violet turned back to Mira. "I'm afraid so, Mira. I would feel terrible if you wore a crown or tiara to dance class and it fell off and broke. It's probably best to save that for playing dress-up at home."

Mira turned around to face her dad. Her father simply shrugged and made a helpless face.

Mira spun back around to face Violet, a big pout on her lips, but there was still determination in her eyes. "What about a *paper* crown?"

There was more laughter from the parents.

Violet liked this child immediately.

"I'll tell you what, Mira. Later in the year we'll have a special dress-up day where everyone can wear their favorite dress-up clothes, including tiaras and crowns. How does that sound?"

The little girl's blue eyes sparkled, and she nodded. "Okay. I like that."

Violet smiled. "Wonderful."

Mira sat back down, spinning around to give her dad a big thumbs up. He returned the gesture in kind.

There was another chime at the front door, followed by commotion. She knew they were going to be late. Jayda didn't get out of school until two thirty, and that was nearly across town.

Her brother Mitch and niece Jayda ran into the studio, both red-faced and out of breath. "Sorry," Mitch mouthed, taking a seat next to Mira's dad. Jayda ran toward the group of children on the floor, one dance shoe on, one dance shoe off. She slid down on her butt next to Mira and proceeded to put on her other slipper.

"Hi, Aunt Violet," she whispered. "Sorry we're late. There was a car accident, and we got stuck in traffic."

"It's okay, sweetheart."

She turned to face the parents along the wall. "There is a waiting room outside for parents, with coffee and tea, but we do ask that you leave the studio during dance practice. We find the children listen better to the dance teacher when their parents are not in the room."

All the parents nodded and slowly started to rise out of their seats, heading toward the doors. All but Mira's dad. He hung back, apprehension in his eyes. Mira wasn't even paying attention to her dad; she was busy talking to Jayda about their matching skirts.

"There is a two-way mirror in the waiting room," Violet said. "So you can see us, but we're not distracted by you."

Mira's dad's bright sapphire eyes, framed by ridiculously long lashes, perked up, and his smile nearly made Violet melt on the spot. "Thanks." Then he left.

She was grateful for Kathleen's suggestion of the two-way mirror, because having Mira's dad in the room was definitely going to be distracting. She hadn't met a man quite so attractive since moving back to Seattle. She hadn't seen a man quite so attractive since Jean-Phillipe.

Guilt and grief stabbed her in the gut at the same time.

Jean-Phillipe.

How could she even think about another man when the love of her life was gone and all that was left of him was his picture hanging in the hallway and his dream of opening up a dance studio?

She couldn't let the pain in her heart cripple her. Not today. Not on opening day. Turning back to the children, she clapped her hands three times and tossed on the biggest smile she could muster. Eventually she wouldn't be faking. Eventually the smile would be real, right?

"All right, children, let's get dancing. Everyone spread out and find some room." She walked over to the big stereo system on the wall and hit the *on* button. Fun, happy, poppy music with a lively beat began to play, and all the children started to move. "Let's get our wiggles out before we start some routines."

Then, pretending to not care, but actually caring a lot that Mira's father was watching them behind the mirror, she did what she did best and let the music take over her body. Let it fill her soul and move her limbs. She didn't have to see him to know he was there. Watching Mira. Watching Violet. And for some reason, she didn't mind. She smiled at the mirror when she came out of her pirouette, made eye contact with the man behind the glass, and for the first time in a very long time, the smile felt real.

BUY IT NOW

https://books2read.com/DWTSD-SDS

## Acknowledgments

There are so many people to thank who help along the way. Publishing a book is definitely not a solo mission, that's for sure. First and foremost, my friend and editor Chris Kridler, you lady are a blessing, a gem and an all-around amazing human being. Thank you for your honesty and hard work.

Thank you, to my critique groups gals, Danielle and Jillian. I love our monthly meet-ups at Starbucks where we give honest feedback and just bitch about life

Andi Babcock for her beta-read, I always appreciate your attention to detail and comments.

Author Jeanne St. James, my alpha reader and sister from another mister, what would I do without you?

Megan J. Parker-Squiers from EmCat Designs, your covers are awesome. Thank you,

My Naughty Room Readers Crew, authors Jeanne St. James, Erica Lynn and Cailin Briste, I love being part of such a tremendous set of inspiring, talented and supportive women. Thank you for letting me learn, lean on and join the team.

My street team, Whitley Cox's Curiously Kinky Reviewers, you are all awesome and I feel so blessed to have found such wonderful fans.

The ladies in Vancouver Island Romance Authors, your support and insight have been incredibly helpful, and I'm so honored to be a part of a group of such talented writers.

Author Cora Seton for you help, tweaks and suggestions for my blurbs, as always, they come back from you so sparkly. I also love our walks, talks and heart-to-hearts, they mean so much to me.

Authors Kathleen Lawless, Nancy Warren and Jane Wallace, I love our writing meetups. Wine, good food and friendship always make the words flow.

The Small Human and the Tiny Human, you are the beats and beasts of my heart, the reason I breathe and the reason I drink. I love you both to infinity and beyond.

And lastly, of course, the husband. You are my forever. I love you.

# OTHER BOOKS BY WHITLEY COX

Love, Passion and Power: Part 1
The Dark and Damaged Hearts Series: Book 1
https://books2read.com/LPP1-DDH
Kendra and Justin

•

Love, Passion and Power: Part 2
The Dark and Damaged Hearts: Book 2
https://books2read.com/LPP2-DDH
Kendra and Justin

•

Sex, Heat and Hunger: Part 1
The Dark and Damaged Hearts Book 3
https://books2read.com/SHH1-DDH
Emma and James

•

Sex, Heat and Hunger: Part 2
The Dark and Damaged Hearts Book 4
https://books2read.com/SHH1-DDH
Emma and James

•

Hot & Filthy: The Honeymoon
The Dark and Damaged Hearts Book 4.5
https://books2read.com/HF-DDH
Emma and James

•

True, Deep and Forever: Part 1
The Dark and Damaged Hearts Book 5
https://books2read.com/TDF1-DDH
Amy and Garrett

•

True, Deep and Forever: Part 2
The Dark and Damaged Hearts Book 6
https://books2read.com/TDF2-DDH
Amy and Garrett

•

Hard, Fast and Madly: Part 1
The Dark and Damaged Hearts Series Book 7
https://books2read.com/HFM1-DDH
Freya and Jacob

•

Hard, Fast and Madly: Part 2
The Dark and Damaged Hearts Series Book 8
https://books2read.com/HFM1-DDH
Freya and Jacob

•

Quick & Dirty
Book 1, A Quick Billionaires Novel
https://books2read.com/QDirty-QBS
Parker and Tate

•

Quick & Easy
Book 2, A Quick Billionaires Novella
https://books2read.com/QEasy-QBS
Heather and Gavin

•

Quick & Reckless
Book 3, A Quick Billionaires Novel
https://books2read.com/QReckless-QBS
Silver and Warren

•

Quick & Dangerous
Book 4, A Quick Billionaires Novel
https://books2read.com/QDangerous-QBS
Skyler and Roberto

•

Quick & Snowy
The Quick Billionaires, Book 5
https://books2read.com/QSnowy-QBS
Brier and Barnes

•

Doctor Smug
https://books2read.com/DoctorSmug
Daisy and Riley

•

Hot Dad
https://books2read.com/Hot-Dad
Harper and Sam

•

Snowed In & Set Up
https://books2read.com/SISU
Amber, Will, Juniper, Hunter, Rowen, Austin

•

Love to Hate You
https://books2read.com/Love2HateYou
Alex and Eli

•

Lust Abroad
https://books2read.com/Lust-Abroad
Piper and Derrick

•

Hired by the Single Dad
https://books2read.com/HBTSD-SDS
The Single Dads of Seattle, Book 1
Tori and Mark

•

Dancing with the Single Dad
https://books2read.com/DWTSD-SDS
The Single Dads of Seattle, Book 2
Violet and Adam

•

Saved by the Single Dad
https://books2read.com/SBTSD-SDS
The Single Dads of Seattle, Book 3
Paige and Mitch

•

Living with the Single Dad
https://books2read.com/LWTSD-SDS
The Single Dads of Seattle, Book 4
Isobel and Aaron

•

Christmas with the Single Dad
https://books2read.com/CWTSD-SDS
The Single Dads of Seattle, Book 5
Aurora and Zak

•

New Year's with the Single Dad
https://books2read.com/NYWTSD-SDS
The Single Dads of Seattle, Book 6
Zara and Emmett

•

Valentine's with the Single Dad
https://books2read.com/VWTSD-SDS
The Single Dads of Seattle, Book 7
Lowenna and Mason

•

Neighbors with the Single Dad
https://books2read.com/NWTSD-SDS
The Single Dads of Seattle, Book 8
Eva and Scott

•

Flirting with the Single Dad
https://books2read.com/FWTSD-SDS
The Single Dads of Seattle, Book 9
Tessa and Atlas

•

Falling for the Single Dad
https://books2read.com/FFTSD-SDS
The Single Dads of Seattle, Book 10
Liam and Richelle

•

Hot for Teacher
https://books2read.com/HFT-SMS
The Single Moms of Seattle, Book1
Celeste and Max

•

Hot for a Cop
https://books2read.com/HFAC-SMS
The Single Moms of Seattle, Book 2
Lauren and Isaac

•

Hot for the Handyman
https://books2read.com/HTHM-SMS
The Single Moms of Seattle, Book 3
Bianca and Jack

•

Mr. Gray Sweatpants
A Single Moms of Seattle spin-off book
https://books2read.com/MrGraySweatpants
Casey and Leo

•

Hard Hart
https://books2read.com/HH-HB
The Harty Boys, Book 1
Krista and Brock

•

Lost Hart
The Harty Boys, Book 2
https://books2read.com/LH-HB
Stacey and Chase

•

Torn Hart
The Harty Boys, Book 3
https://books2read.com/THART-HB
Lydia and Rex

•

Dark Hart
The Harty Boys, Book 4
https://books2read.com/DH-HB
Pasha and Heath

•

Full Hart
The Harty Boys, Book 5
https://books2read.com/FH-HB
A Harty Boys Family Christmas
Joy and Grant

•

Not Over You
A Young Sisters Novel
https://books2read.com/not-over-you
Rayma and Jordan

Snowed in with the Rancher
A Young Sisters Novel
https://books2read.com/snowed-in-rancher
Triss and Asher
March 4, 2023
•
Second Chance with the Rancher
A Young Sisters Novel
https://books2read.com/second-chance-rancher
Mieka and Nate
May 13, 2023
•
Done with You
A Young Sisters Novel
https://books2read.com/done-with-you
Oona and Aiden
October 13, 2023
•
Rock the Shores
A Cinnamon Bay Romance
https://books2read.com/Rocktheshores
Juliet and Evan
•
The Bastard Heir
Winter Harbor Heroes, Book 1
Co-written with Ember Leigh
https://books2read.com/the-bastard-heir
Harlow and Callum
•
The Asshole Heir
Winter Harbor Heroes, Book 2
Co-written with Ember Leigh
https://books2read.com/the-asshole-heir
Amaya and Carson

The Rebel Heir
Winter Harbor Heroes, Book 3
Co-written with Ember Leigh
https://books2read.com/the-rebel-heir
Lily and Colton
March 18, 2023

## NATALIE SLOAN TITLES

Light the Fire
Revolution Inferno, Book 1
https://mybook.to/light-the-fire
Haina, Zane, Alaric and Jorik

•

Stoke the Flames
Revolution Inferno, Book 2
https://mybook.to/stoke-the-flames
Olia, Maxxon, Cypher and Alaric

•

Burn it Down
Revolution Inferno, Book 3
https://mybook.to/burn-it-down
Zosha, Knox, Shade and Tozer
June 3, 2023

# ABOUT THE AUTHOR

A Canadian West Coast baby born and raised, Whitley is married to her high school sweetheart, and together they have two beautiful daughters and a fluffy dog. She spends her days making food that gets thrown on the floor, vacuuming Cheerios out from under the couch and making sure that the dog food doesn't end up in the air conditioner. But when nap time comes, and it's not quite wine o'clock, Whitley sits down, avoids the pile of laundry on the couch, and writes. A lover of all things decadent; wine, cheese, chocolate and spicy erotic romance, Whitley brings the humorous side of sex, the ridiculous side of relationships and the suspense of everyday life into her stories. With single dads, firefighters, Navy SEALs, mommy wars, body issues, threesomes, bondage and role-playing, Whitley's books have all the funny and fabulously filthy words you could hope for.

Website: WhitleyCox.com
Email: readers4wcox@gmail.com
Twitter: @WhitleyCoxBooks
Instagram: @CoxWhitley
TikTok: @AuthorWhitleyCox
Facebook : https://www.facebook.com/CoxWhitley/
Blog: https://whitleycox.com/fabulously-filthy-blog-page/

Exclusive Facebook Reader Group:
https://www.facebook.com/groups/234716323653592/
Booksprout: https://booksprout.co/author/994/whitley-cox
Bookbub: https://www.bookbub.com/authors/whitley-cox
Goodreads:
https://www.goodreads.com/author/show/16344419.Whitley_Cox
Subscribe to my newsletter here:
http://eepurl.com/ckh5yT

*Treat yourself to awesome orgasms!*
*This one only ships to the US.*

https://tracysdog.com/?sca_ref=1355619.ybw0YXuvPL

*Treat yourself to awesome orgasms! This one ships to Canada!*

https://thornandfeather.ca/?ref=734ThbSs

Made in the USA
Middletown, DE
19 March 2024

51740289R00130